TARAH'S LESSONS

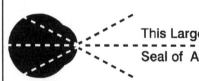

This Large Print Book carries the
Seal of Approval of N.A.V.H.

KANSAS HOME, BOOK 2

Tarah's Lessons

A HEART ADRIFT FINDS A PLACE TO DWELL IN THIS ROMANTIC STORY

Lp
BAt

2008

JUL

Tracey V. Bateman

THORNDIKE PRESS
A part of Gale, Cengage Learning

GALE
CENGAGE Learning™

Detroit • New York • San Francisco • New Haven, Conn • Waterville, Maine • London

GALE
CENGAGE Learning

LIBRARY OF CONGRESS CATALOGING-IN-PUBLICATION DATA

Bateman, Tracey Victoria
   Tarah's lessons : a heart adrift finds a place to dwell in this romantic story / by Tracey V. Bateman.
      p. cm. — (Kansas home ; bk. 2) (Thorndike Press large print Christian romance)
      ISBN-13: 978-1-4104-0760-3 (hardcover : alk. paper)
      ISBN-10: 1-4104-0760-8 (hardcover : alk. paper)
      1. Large type books. I. Title.
   PS3602.A854T37 2008
   813'.6—dc22   2008011506

Published in 2008 by arrangement with Barbour Publishing, Inc.

Printed in the United States of America
1 2 3 4 5 6 7 12 11 10 09 08

*Lovingly dedicated to my four children:
Cat, Michael, Stevan, and Will.
You'll learn so many lessons throughout
your precious lives, lessons taught by
scores of teachers.
But the most important, by far, are those
taught by a loving Father as He molds
you into the vessels He created you to
be.
My prayer is that you will learn the
lessons well.
Mommy loves you.
Special thanks to Chris Lynxwiler and my
mom, Frances Devine, who have each
read this book so many times for editing
purposes, they must know it by heart.*

CHAPTER 1

1871

Tarah St. John stood at the doorway of the little sod schoolhouse and waved good-bye to her departing students. Finally the endless day was over!

Releasing a weary sigh, she pressed her palms to her cheeks and rubbed vigorously, attempting to ease her aching jaw. Whoever had said that "a smile never hurt anyone" had obviously never tried to force one all day.

With purpose, she pulled the wooden door firmly shut and turned to her one remaining student. She narrowed her gaze, set her lips into a firm line, and stomped back to the front of the room, her blue gingham skirt swishing about her legs.

Very near to tears, Tarah rammed her hands on her hips and faced the red-headed boy writing sentences on the slate blackboard. "Luke St. John," she said furiously, "you just wait 'til Pa hears about this."

"Aw," her twelve-year-old brother protested, keeping his eyes on the task at hand, "you ain't gotta tell Ma and Pa."

"I don't *have* to tell them," she corrected. "But it just so happens I want to. Honestly, your orneriness is probably the sole reason Miss Nelson gave up teaching and hightailed it back east." She paced the floor behind him, trying to come up with just the right words to make him thoroughly ashamed of himself.

"Come on, Tarah." He kicked at the ground with a booted toe. "Don't be mad."

Steeling herself against his conciliatory tone, Tarah glared at her brother. She refused to let him off the hook so easily. "You made me look plumb foolish, Luke. Did you have to show off for the new girl on my very first day of teaching?"

Luke stopped his nearly illegible scrawling and turned to her, his green eyes flashing in anger. "I weren't showing off for no girl!"

"*Wasn't* showing off for *any* girl. And you were so. I saw you staring at Josie Raney all during spelling lessons this morning. And from the looks of those sentences," she said with a pointed glance at the board, "you need to concentrate on spelling a sight more than you need to look at a pretty new face.

8

There are two *b*'s in *ribbons*."

"I *wasn't* looking at her pretty face," Luke insisted.

Tarah couldn't resist a teasing grin. "So you *do* think she's pretty."

Caught by his own words, the boy grinned back, showing teeth still rather large for his face. He shrugged. "I reckon."

"Then why in the world did you dip her ribbon in your inkwell? Don't you know they cost money?"

Luke shifted and stared at his feet. "Guess I weren't thinking about that," he mumbled.

"Apparently you *weren't*," Tarah said with a sniff. "Well, you'll just have to buy her a new one."

Panic sparked in the boy's eyes. "But I don't got no money."

She lifted a delicate brow and regarded him frankly. "I suppose I'd be willing to help you out."

"You would?" Hope widened Luke's eyes.

Tarah nodded. "I'll give you a penny a day until you have enough to pay for the ribbons. But you'll have to earn it."

She felt a prick of guilt about bribing him, but after the day he'd put her through, she was just weary enough to offer him anything. If he would just be good until the other children got used to her, his disruptions would be manageable. As it was, he only encouraged unruly behavior among the other students.

Suspicion clouded the hope in his eyes. "What do I gotta do?"

"All you *have* to do is be good in class."

Luke's eyebrows darted upward. "That's it?"

Tarah bit back the smile threatening the corners of her mouth. She knew her brother. He would definitely have to work hard to earn that money. "That's all. Think you can manage it?"

He scrunched his nose, obviously trying to weigh his options. "How much do hair ribbons cost?"

"Five cents ought to get her enough ribbon for a matched pair."

"Two? But I only inked one of her ol' ribbons."

"Yes, but she was wearing a matching set. One of which you ruined. A girl can't go around wearing two different-colored ribbons in her hair."

Luke's shoulders slumped in defeat, and he turned back to writing his sentences. "Aw, who cares if they match anyway?" he muttered.

"She does," Tarah replied firmly. "And so do I. Do we have a deal?"

A heavy sigh escaped his lips. "I guess I don't got no choice."

"Good." Elated by the victory, Tarah didn't even bother to correct his grammar. "I'll buy the ribbon on the way home from school, and all you have to do is behave yourself for a week."

He scowled and nodded.

"Now hurry and finish those sentences so we can get home and help with chores."

Breathing a sigh of relief, Tarah turned and began to tidy up the books scattered across her desk.

The door opened just then, and sunlight streamed into the small schoolhouse. Tarah glanced up as Josie Raney shuffled to the front of the room.

"Why, Josie, did you forget something?"

A deep chuckle emanated from the doorway. "My niece forgot her little brother, I'm afraid."

Tarah squinted against the blinding light, trying to make out the man's features. She caught her breath as he stepped through the doorway into plain view. Anthony Greene. Looking every bit as handsome as ever. He still had the same unruly sandy blond hair and brown eyes, able to melt a girl's insides with one glance in her direction — like now. "Why, Anthony," she said breathlessly. "When did you get back in town?"

"Hello, Tarah." He grinned broadly. "So you *are* the new schoolteacher. I thought Ma was pulling my leg."

Tarah bristled. "Why's that? Don't you think I can be a teacher?" After the day she had just gone through, she wasn't at all sure she could be a teacher, but she certainly didn't need anyone else questioning the fact.

"Sure," he said with a lift of his brow. "I just figured some lucky man would have married you by now."

Heat rose to her cheeks as memories of her schoolgirl crush came rushing back to torture her. She'd had dreams of marrying *him.* But one year her senior, Anthony Greene was the only young man in Harper who had seemed unaware she existed. Much to Tarah's humiliation, he'd preferred the simpering Louisa Thomas.

When he'd left for seminary, no one had expected he'd ever be back. But there he was, as real as Luke's big, ornery, knowing grin.

"Hi, Anthony," Luke said, stepping forward with an outstretched hand. "We've missed you." Tilting his head, he gave Tarah a sly look from the corner of his eye. "Haven't we, sis?"

The lilt in his voice sent a warning through Tarah. Surely he was not going to humiliate her in front of Anthony Greene, of all people!

"Luke . . . ," Tarah warned.

"My hand's awfully tired from writing those sentences, Tarah." Luke's voice rang with challenge.

The boy would pay and pay dearly. "All right," she replied through gritted teeth, taking care to keep what she hoped to be a sweet smile plastered on her face. "I think you've learned your lesson." She'd deal with the little stinker later. Right now she had to thwart any embarrassing comment he might make about her former crush.

"Now," she said, turning her attention back to Anthony and Josie. "What's this about Toby not making it home with you?" she asked the girl.

"I thought he was right behind me," Josie replied, keeping her gaze on the floor.

"I know where he is," Luke spoke up. "I saw him go to the outhouse."

Josie's chin jerked upward, and she stared wide-eyed at Luke.

He cleared his throat. "Yeah, I . . . uh . . . saw him through the window when I was writing sentences."

"And you didn't see him come out?"

Anthony asked incredulously.

Luke kept his gaze fixed on Josie's pale face. "Naw," he said with a shrug. "But that old latch is rusty. It gets stuck all the time. Don't it, Tarah?"

"Doesn't it," she corrected. "And Pa just fixed it last week."

"I'd better go check on him," Anthony said. "Come along, Jo."

"I think I'll stay in here and help Luke clean the blackboard," Josie said, giving Anthony a sweet smile. "If that's okay with you, Uncle Anthony."

A flood of color rushed to Luke's cheeks, making his freckles pop out even brighter. "I don't need no —"

"How sweet of you," Tarah broke in, pleasantly surprised by the kind gesture. Maybe Luke's crush on this girl would prove to be a motivating factor for improving his behavior. One could certainly hope, anyway.

Tarah observed Anthony's broad shoulders as he headed toward the door. Her heartbeat quickened, and she hurried to follow him. It was only natural for her to make sure the little boy made it home all right, she inwardly insisted. Her concern had nothing whatsoever to do with a desire to prolong her contact with Anthony. Oh, who was she trying to fool? Anthony had walked out of her life when he'd left town two years ago without so much as a backward glance, and she had no intention of letting it happen again!

"So you're the new teacher. . . ."

"I didn't know you had a niece and nephew. . . ."

They spoke together as they walked around the side of the building.

Tarah laughed. "You first."

He gave a deep chuckle, the pleasant sound causing Tarah's stomach to do somersaults.

"They're my sister Ella's kids," he explained. "She and her husband, Joe, stayed back east when Pa moved the family out here three years ago."

"So your sister and brother-in-law decided to move out here after all?"

He shook his head. "Only Ella and the children came. They'll stay and help Ma for a while. Pa's death was awfully hard on her."

"Oh, Anthony, how thoughtless of me. I'm terribly sorry about your pa's passing."

Anthony swallowed hard and nodded. "It was a shock. If I had known he was ill, I never would have left."

Tarah reached out and gently touched his arm. "You mustn't blame yourself," she said softly. "There was no way you or anyone else could possibly have known."

He stopped walking and turned to her, covering her hand with his own. "Thank you, Tarah," he said earnestly. "I guess I know that in my heart. But I can't help but feel if I had been here to take on some of the load, his heart wouldn't have given out the way it did."

Tarah opened her mouth to reply but stopped short as a cry broke through the moment.

"L–l–let me out. I w–w–want out."

Together, Tarah and Anthony sprinted the few final yards to the outhouse.

The door was more than jammed. Someone had wrapped a rope around the entire outhouse, obviously locking the little boy in there on purpose.

"Honestly," Tarah said. "Who would have done such a thing?"

Anthony tossed a quick glance toward the schoolhouse. "I think I have a pretty good idea," he drawled.

He quickly untied the simple knot and unwound the rope. The door swung open, and six-year-old Toby stumbled out of the doorway. Fat tears rolled down his chubby cheeks as he grabbed on to Anthony's legs and hung on for all he was worth.

Tarah knelt beside the boy. "Sweetie, who did this?"

"J–j–jo," he said, then dissolved into tears once more.

"You mean your sister, Josie?" she asked incredulously.

"Uh-huh. She said n–n–no one w–w–would miss me and I'd b–b–be here all n–n–night."

Anthony lifted his nephew and held him close. "Well, someone did miss you, scout," he soothed. "As soon as Jo came home alone, your ma sent me looking for you."

"M–m–ma still wants me?" The little boy pulled slightly away and looked at Anthony with wide, hopeful eyes. "Even w–w–with the n–n–new b–baby coming?"

"Of course she does. Who could ever replace our Toby?"

"Jo s–s–said sh–sh–she wants a b–b–boy wh–who d–d–doesn't st–st–stutter."

Indignation filled Tarah. So much for her idea that the girl would be a good influence on Luke. Imagine making the tyke feel as though he were about to be replaced — then locking him in the outhouse to boot.

Anthony disentangled himself from Toby's death grip and set the boy gently on the ground. "You ready to go, scout? Your ma's pretty worried about you. We should go and let her know you're all right."

Toby bobbed his head and swiped at his nose with the back of his hand.

Tarah grimaced as he slipped the same hand inside Anthony's. To her amazement, Anthony smiled affectionately at his nephew and tightened his grip. "Then let's get your sister and go home. You coming, Tarah?"

"In a moment. I think I need to get this rope to a safe place so we don't have a repeat of this incident."

"All right, then. I'm going to round up Jo and head for home. And, Tarah . . ."

"Yes?"

He held her with a long, penetrating gaze, sending her pulse racing. "Thanks for listening to me about . . . you know."

Exhaling slowly, Tarah nodded but couldn't find the appropriate response. He hesitated for a moment, then gave her another heart-stopping smile and turned to go back to the school.

Honestly, Tarah berated herself as the words she should have said spilled into her mind. *Couldn't you have at least said something? Anything would have been better than staring at him like he had dirt on his nose.*

Shaking her head in disgust, she bent forward and picked up the rope from where it still lay in a tangled mess in front of the outhouse. When she stood up, she caught movement from the corner of her eye. Through the window, she saw Luke and Jo — each doubled over in laughter.

Tarah wasn't sure if they were laughing at her or at the cruel joke Josie had played on her brother, but either way she felt the heat rush to her cheeks. She groaned aloud. Not only did she have Luke to contend with — now he had an ally.

Anthony excused himself from the uproar following his homecoming with the two children. That niece of his was a perfect terror, he decided as he walked out the door to the barn. Thankfully chores waited to be done, so he wouldn't be able to hear her howls from the much-deserved whipping she was about to receive.

Poor Tarah! As the schoolteacher, she would have her hands full with Josie, and if her own brother Luke was anything like he used to be, she'd be lucky to stick it out for the whole term.

A grin lifted the corners of his mouth as he stepped inside the barn. That Tarah St. John was still just about the prettiest thing he'd ever laid eyes on. He would have asked for permission to court her years ago, but just when he thought she might agree to such a thing, he'd felt an urge to go to seminary, an urge he knew was from God and too strong to ignore.

He drew in the pungent odor of fresh hay combined with manure. Returning to farm life hadn't exactly been in his plans after he'd accepted the call to preach. He had headed back east to seminary with the intention of returning home only to visit his family. But he knew better than to question God.

"Lord," he prayed while mucking out the first stall, "I know my responsibility is to Ma and the boys." He released a heavy sigh. "I don't begrudge them the help, but sometimes I feel like if I don't get the chance to preach, I'm going to explode."

He cast a sidelong glance at the barn door to make sure he was alone, then turned to the black gelding finishing his supper.

"For God so loved the world," he told Dodger, his faithful four-legged parishioner, "that He gave."

With a complete lack of interest, the horse stamped a hoof on the barn floor and swished his tail at a fly.

"The Lord gave all He had so that you . . . yes," he said, pointing a finger at the long face, "I mean *you,* could have eternal life."

Anthony felt the excitement surge within

him, and he dropped the pitchfork. Pacing the barn, he included all the pitifully sinful creatures with a wide sweep of his hand.

"Now if Jesus gave His life — a sacrifice on an altar made by sinful, greedy men — do you dare keep yourself back from His free gift of salvation? Salvation bought with the blood of God's innocent Son?"

Sweat began to bead on his forehead.

"Must the Lord strive forever with man?"

His voice rose to match the excitement of his eloquent message. June, the milk cow, raised her head and stared, clearly captivated by the rousing sermon. Anthony focused on the sorrowful brown eyes gazing back at him. "Oh, wicked and sinful generation, will you harden your hearts forever, or will you return to your God with weeping and a rending of hearts?"

"Uncle Anthony?"

Rats! Just when he was about to give the altar call!

He turned to face Josie. "I thought you were in trouble."

She shrugged. "Ma whipped me."

Must not have made much of an impression, Anthony thought wryly, for the little girl's face held an impish grin.

"What are you doing out here? Come to help muck out the barn?"

21

A wrinkle creased the perky little nose. "Uh-uh. Ma says I should come talk to you so you can tell me how a Christian girl is supposed to treat others."

"I see." A grin tipped the corners of his mouth. A captive audience.

Josie tilted her blond head to one side and regarded him frankly. "Yeah. But I figure it'll save us both a heap of trouble if we just forget about it and tell her you gave it to me good."

"Josie! That would be a lie."

She released a long-suffering sigh. "Oh, all right. But can we make it short? Reverend Cahill back home used to yak and yak and yak until I almost fell asleep."

Troubled by his niece's lack of reverence, Anthony grabbed a horse blanket from a peg on the wall and spread it out on the barn floor. "Sit yourself down on this blanket, little girl, before I tan your hide."

Anthony "yakked" about kindness and mentioned every fruit of the Spirit from Galatians chapter five while he finished cleaning the barn. Hanging the pitchfork high on the wall, he added a mention of the Golden Rule to his lecture for good measure.

"All right. I think that's enough for tonight." He glanced at Josie. "Let's go inside for supper."

With a sleepy yawn, the little girl stood.

Anthony shook his head. He doubted she'd heard a word of his exhortation any more than the animals had heard his brilliant sermon.

"Uncle Anthony?" Josie asked as they headed back to the house.

"Yeah?"

She looked up at him, her angelic face filled with question. Her eyes serious, she shook her head sadly.

Anthony's heart leapt. Maybe he'd made an impression after all. "What is it, sweetheart?"

"Well, I was just wondering . . ."

"Yes?"

"Do you think there's any hope for that poor cow's soul?" Merriment filled her eyes as she giggled and dashed off across the yard.

"Why, you little . . ." Anthony followed her. "You'd better run, you little stinker. When I catch you, I'm going to tickle you until you recite all the books of the Bible . . . backwards."

CHAPTER 2

Tarah set a platter laden with golden fried chicken on the lacy tablecloth covering a long, wooden table. She bent and gave her father a kiss on the cheek, then took her seat.

Grateful to be back in familiar surroundings after her harrowing first day of teaching, Tarah smiled at her ten-year-old sister, Emily, sitting to her right. The family members joined hands in preparation for their mealtime prayer.

Pa's gaze roved around the table and settled on Ma's bowed head. "Cassidy?"

Cassidy glanced up, her wide green eyes filled with question.

"Where's Sam?"

"He asked permission to eat supper with Camilla and her family. I didn't think you'd mind."

An amused glance passed between them.

Pa sent Tarah a teasing wink. "Looks like

we might be attending Sam's wedding before his big sister's if she doesn't stop sending those young men away."

Tarah gasped.

"Dell!" Ma frowned and shook her head.

"What?"

"It—it's okay, Ma." But Pa's comment stung and only proved a painful reminder to Tarah that she was nineteen years old with no prospects for marriage. She felt her defenses rise. Was it her fault all the boys she'd admired in school had grown up to be dolts? Well, all except Anthony.

Ma stared pointedly at Pa. "Let's just say the prayer, shall we?" she suggested.

Pa shrugged, still wearing a confused frown. Finally he bowed his dark head and prayed. "Father, we thank You for the many blessings You've given this growing family. We ask You to watch over Mother while she's away visiting George and Olive. Thank You for Tarah's new teaching position. May You give her wisdom to teach with grace and patience." He cleared his throat. "And we thank You for the new blessing You are bringing into our lives. A new baby for us to love and . . ."

Emily squealed and leaped from her chair. "Ma!"

"Emily St. John!" Cassidy scolded. "Your

pa's praying."

"I'm sorry," she whispered and slowly returned to her seat.

Pa grinned. "In Jesus' name, amen."

Emily's carrot-orange braids flew behind her as she sprinted around the table and grabbed Ma, hugging her tightly.

Luke's face glowed bright red, and he gave Pa a sheepish grin. "Another baby, huh?" He jerked a thumb toward the twins sitting in high chairs on either side of Ma. "Just when those two were starting to grow up and not cry all the time."

Tarah noticed her stepmother's eyes cloud over with hurt until Luke gave her a wide grin. "Hope it's a boy!"

A relieved smile curved Ma's lips. "I'll see what I can do."

Feeling her father's gaze upon her, Tarah rose and embraced her stepmother, then her pa. "Congratulations," she murmured. "This is wonderful news." She sank back in her chair.

"Can we name him Pete?" All eyes turned to Jack. Even at seven years old, his soft brown eyes and mop of unruly curls gave him an angelic appearance.

"That's a dumb name," Emily said haughtily, still standing close to Cassidy. "Besides, it's going to be a girl, and we'll call her Audra."

"Pete!"

"Audra!"

"That's enough, you two," Pa said firmly. "There'll be plenty of time to discuss names later on. Right now you'd better sit down so we can eat this supper your ma cooked before it gets cold."

The revelation that Cassidy was expecting another child came as no surprise to Tarah, who, as the eldest of seven children, had recognized the symptoms in her stepmother over the past couple of months. She wasn't unhappy about the coming baby, but the house was getting cramped as it was. With trees so scarce, Pa and the boys would have to haul sandstone from the river to build on to the house.

Lord, it would be a lot easier all the way around if You would just send me a husband. One or two of the kids could have my room. You know, Anthony Greene came back. . . .

She stopped, uncomfortable with the thought that she might be trying to manipulate the Lord.

Well, she wasn't exactly telling God something He didn't already know. *Besides,* she reasoned, *maybe God sent Anthony back here so we could be married. It never hurts to ask.*

She bit into a slice of buttered bread and tried to focus on what Pa was saying.

"How was your first day, Teacher?" Pa grabbed a piece of fried chicken from the platter and sent Tarah a proud grin.

"Anthony Greene showed up after school," Luke piped in before Tarah could swallow her food and answer.

The bread lodged in her throat, and she coughed profusely while Emily pounded her on the back.

"Tarah," Ma said, "are you all right?"

Nodding, she grabbed her water glass to wash down the mouthful of bread, sending Luke a warning glance over the rim.

He raised his eyebrows and sent her one right back.

Tarah's temper flared. So that was how he wanted to play it. If she mentioned his unruly behavior, he'd tease her about Anthony in front of the whole family. At least Sam was off having supper with Camilla Simpson and her family, or the temptation might have been too great for Luke to resist despite their agreement.

Over a barrel, she drew a deep breath and decided to let it slide. After all, she had his promise of good behavior for a whole week.

A promise he'd better keep if he knew what was good for him.

Apparently oblivious to the silent exchange between his children, Pa pointed his empty fork at no one in particular and gave a reflective frown. He glanced at Tarah. "Anthony went to seminary back east, didn't he?"

Tarah nodded, glad the focus was off her disappointing first day of teaching.

"What are you thinking, Dell?" Ma asked.

Tarah looked from one to the other. The love evident in their eyes for each other sent a small ache to her heart. Would she ever find someone to love? With Anthony's return to Harper, her prospects seemed to be looking up. *But only if it's Your will,* she added hastily.

"Well, my darling," Pa said with a grin, "I was thinking we just might have us a preacher."

Ma clapped her hands together, causing the nearly two-year-old twins, Hope and Will, to do the same. "What a wonderful idea!"

"I'll talk it over with the rest of the council at the meeting tonight," Pa said. "And if they agree, I'll probably swing by the Greene farm on the way home. So I might be a little later than usual." He winked at Tarah.

"Think you'd mind sharing the schoolhouse with the preacher for Sunday services, little teacher?"

"Tarah wouldn't mind sharing . . . ," Luke began.

Tarah shot him another warning glance.

"Of course she won't mind," Ma said, wiping a glob of potatoes from baby Will's plump chin.

Anthony . . . to be the new preacher. Tarah's heart skipped a beat, and she released a dreamy sigh. What would it be like to be a preacher's wife?

Tarah watched proudly as Anthony strode to the rough-hewn wooden pulpit, normally used only twice a year when the circuit rider came through. She'd waited nearly a week to see him again.

Dressed in a black coat, black trousers, and a white shirt, he looked awfully handsome. She smiled at his crooked tie. Once they were married, she'd take care of that little problem for him.

Tarah caught her breath when he looked directly at her as though guessing her thoughts. Almost sure that wasn't possible, she nevertheless felt herself blush to the roots of her hair. Anthony's gaze moved past her, sweeping the congregation. His Adam's apple bobbed up and down as he swallowed hard.

Say something, Anthony.

She watched in concern as his face paled. He grabbed on to the pulpit, his knuckles growing instantly white.

Oh no, he's going to pass out cold!

A gust of cool autumn wind blew into the little schoolhouse-turned-church as the door swung open. Tarah noticed Anthony relax visibly as the latecomer turned the congregation's attention from him to the back of the room.

He looked at her again. Tarah nodded encouragement and returned his smile. "You can do it," she mouthed. She pointed upward, hoping to remind him God would be his helper. His grin widened, and he nodded back to her, then cleared his throat to regain the congregation's attention.

"Excuse me," someone whispered from the aisle next to Tarah.

Irritated to have her attention drawn away from Anthony, Tarah glanced up. Louisa Thomas. What did *she* want?

"May I sit next to you?" the young woman whispered. "There's nowhere else."

Tarah cast a furtive glance around the tiny room, hoping to spy an empty seat and send her on her way. When her search proved futile, she sighed and scooted over.

"I'm so glad I didn't miss Anthony's sermon. Doesn't he look marvelous?" Louisa whispered. "It was worth getting up early to watch him for an hour."

Jealousy stabbed at Tarah's heart. She frowned. "Shh."

Louisa didn't even have the grace to blush for disrupting the service. She looked at Anthony and gave him a broad you-may-begin-now smile.

Temper flaring, Tarah inched a little farther away from the bothersome flirt and bumped into old Mr. Moody, already nodding off on the other side of her. He jerked his head up. "Thanks, little lady," he said aloud, sending her a wink. "Do that again next time you hear me snoring."

The building rumbled with muffled laughter.

Humiliated, Tarah sank down in her seat. *It would be a mercy if the floor would open up and swallow me right now, Lord.*

Anthony cleared his throat again.

Finally!

"Thank you all for coming," Anthony began in a shaky voice. "I'd like to begin with a word of prayer."

Relieved for the chance to close her eyes and shake off the embarrassment, Tarah bowed her head.

"Oh, most precious heavenly Father," he began, dropping his voice at least two notches. "We thank Thee for the opportunity to assemble together in Thy most holy presence."

Tarah frowned. Was it her imagination, or was he trying to be impressive in his prayer? She felt a niggling disappointment creep through her.

People were beginning to shuffle when he finally said "amen" a good five minutes later.

Breathing a sigh of relief, Tarah waited for the sermon to begin. Anthony glanced at his notes for a minute, took a long, slow breath, then stared gravely from the pulpit.

"For God so loved the world," he began, "that He gave . . ."

The tension eased away from Tarah's shoulders, and she felt herself relaxing.

His voice strengthened. "Now if God gave His only Son — a sacrifice on the altar of sinful and greedy men — do you *dare* keep yourself back from His free gift of salvation?"

The flimsy pulpit shook as Anthony's hand slapped down hard on the wooden surface.

Tarah started at the suddenness of the action. Beside her, Old Man Moody jerked his chin from his chest. "What? Amen, Preacher!"

Louisa giggled, starting a chain reaction throughout the room, and soon everyone was laughing.

Anthony's face turned a deep shade of red, and he glanced back down at his notes. When the laughter died, he eyed the congregation and continued as though nothing had occurred. "Salvation bought with the blood of God's innocent Son?"

"You ever see a person sweat that much before?" ten-year-old Emily asked that afternoon at dinner.

"Emily," Ma admonished, "don't be rude."

But Tarah noticed that Ma placed a napkin to her mouth to hide her smile.

"I saw Mr. Gordon sweat worse than that during harvest last year," Luke offered. " 'Course, that was before Doc Simpson made him lose all that fat. I thought ol' Anthony was going to start dripping on the floor."

"Luke!" Ma said, now nearly choking to keep from laughing aloud.

Pa's blue eyes twinkled. "He did get quite a lather going, didn't he?"

Unable to suppress her mirth any longer,

34

Ma laughed until tears rolled down her cheeks. Pa threw back his head and joined her. And of course, the children couldn't resist.

Sam slapped his hand down on the table, sending half of the utensils flying. " 'You,' " he said, lowering his voice in imitation of Anthony — a very poor imitation, in Tarah's opinion. " 'I mean *you!*' "

Tarah stared at her family with indignation. "I thought Anthony did a fine job," she said with a toss of her head.

The room suddenly grew quiet as her family stared at her, each face registering the same look of disbelief.

Looking around the table, Tarah released a sigh of concession. "Oh, all right. So he didn't do that great. But honestly, it *was* his first time to preach."

Ma sobered, her gaze searching Tarah's face. Her expression softened, and her lips curved in a smile of understanding.

Unable to abide the scrutiny, Tarah felt her cheeks flush as she averted her gaze and studied the blue-flowered print on her plate.

"Tarah's right," Ma said. "We have to give Anthony a chance to find his own preaching style. I'm sure next week will be better."

"I sure hope so," Luke said, shoving a bite of roasted venison into his mouth. "But I'm bringing a bucket to put under him just in case."

But the next week wasn't an improvement. Neither was the week after, nor the week after that. By the time Anthony had been there a month, the good folks of Harper, Kansas, were beginning to grumble about the hellfire-and-brimstone preacher.

Anthony awoke with a looming sense of dread. Maybe he could pretend to be sick this morning. His stomach *was* feeling a mite queasy at the thought of facing his unresponsive congregation once again.

He lay in the predawn stillness, his silent pleas stretching from his heart to God's.

Why won't they listen, Lord?

Sometimes he felt like Noah must have, knowing the flood was coming and the people weren't ready. The cows and horses paid more attention to his sermons than his shrinking congregation ever did. And he'd noticed people were beginning to avoid him like a bad smell. Everyone but Louisa Thomas. She seemed to genuinely appreciate his messages. Her smiling face was the highlight of his Sunday mornings.

With a heavy sigh, Anthony drew back the covers and sat at the edge of his bed, trying to muster the enthusiasm to get up and begin the new day.

"This is the day which the Lord has made. I will rejoice and be glad in it," he muttered, feeling anything but joyful. Willing himself to move, he stood and walked barefoot across the small room, poured water into a basin, and grabbed his razor.

A groan escaped his lips as he caught his reflection in the mirror. Even with the overnight scruff of a beard and mustache on his face, he looked like a teenage boy. No wonder no one took him seriously.

Rats! What could he do about his face? He stared into the mirror, wishing for distinguishing gray at his temples or maybe a few lines on his face to indicate wisdom beyond his years. Pushing away the ludicrous train of thought, Anthony sighed and set down his razor. At the very least, he would allow his beard and mustache to grow. That would make him look older.

With that decision made, he dressed quickly and headed to the kitchen, following the heady aroma of bacon frying and biscuits baking in the oven.

"Morning, Ma," he said, bending to plant a kiss on her weathered cheek. He drank in the comfortingly familiar scents of lemon verbena combined with dough.

"Morning, son." She directed him to a

chair with a nod of her head. "Blane says not to worry about chores this morning. He was up early and finished."

"That's a blessing." Anthony sank into a chair at the end of the table and stretched out his legs, leaning back in his chair. "Where is he?"

"Cleaning up. He should be in here soon." Ma grabbed a cup from the shelf above the counter. "Coffee?"

Anthony nodded absently. "Thanks," he said and looked up with a smile as she set the steaming cup in front of him.

"Something troubling you, son?"

Breathing a heavy sigh, he waved a hand and shook his head. "Nothing anyone but God can help me with, I'm afraid." Right now, he'd welcome a good talk with his mentor from his church back east. But Reverend Cahill was too far away to be of any help.

"I just don't know what these folks expect."

Ma removed the bacon from the skillet and set it on a platter. "I don't think they expect much, Anthony," she said thoughtfully.

Surprised, Anthony shot a glance at his mother. He hadn't meant to speak aloud.

Setting the platter on the table, Ma stared

down at him with a tender smile. "They just want to hear the Word preached with love and authority from someone who knows the heart of God."

Well, that pretty well summed him up, he figured. He loved these people enough to be concerned for their eternal souls and preached with so much authority that it took him all Sunday afternoon to recover from the exertion.

He preached what he had been taught to preach: Show the people their sin, and give them the opportunity to repent. Surely that was the heart of God. Still, if that were the case, why wasn't he seeing positive results?

"I don't know, Ma," he said. "Seems to me the congregation is half the size it started out to be. If I don't do something, I'll lose the rest of them, too." Then he'd be asked to leave at the end of the three-month trial period. The thought of failing clenched his gut.

Ma rested a thoughtful gaze upon him. "Have you prayed about this?"

Raking his fingers through his hair, Anthony released a long, slow breath. "I pray constantly for the people in this town. I've never seen such an unresponsive group." He met her gaze, suddenly feeling the need to unload his frustration. "Do you know the people who have stopped coming to the services are meeting out at the Johnsons' place on Sunday mornings?" It cut him to the core and more than wounded his pride that the folks would opt to share the Word among themselves rather than come to his services.

"I heard something about that." Ma's voice held a twinge of sympathy as she sat and gave his hand a gentle pat. "You just have to concentrate on the members of your flock and not worry about those who feel they need to meet elsewhere."

"I reckon you're right. Still, it's puzzling."

"I don't want to be telling you your business, son, but it might do some good for you to get to know the members of your congregation better."

"What do you mean?"

She shrugged, and her pensive gaze held his. "Seems to me I hear an awful lot of folks inviting you to Sunday dinner, and yet you're always right here at my table."

Anthony shot her a wide grin. "Why should I go eat somewhere else when the best cook in Kansas is right here in my own home?"

"Oh, now. You stop exaggerating." But her eyes crinkled at the corners for an instant before she grew serious once again. "I just think maybe folks would like a chance to visit with you outside of the church. Let them get to know the real Anthony instead of just Reverend Greene."

The thought had never occurred to him before, but as he rolled the idea around, it seemed to make sense. "You think that might make a difference?" Anthony almost cringed at the desperation in his voice.

"Couldn't hurt. People want to know their minister cares about their everyday lives and not just their spiritual condition. Remember, the Bible states that Jesus ate with His disciples. He washed their feet and answered all of their questions. Tending sheep is much more than just feeding and watering."

"Ma, sometimes I think you should have been the preacher and not me." He drained his cup and stood.

"Where do you think you're going? You haven't had your breakfast yet."

He flashed her another grin, feeling more lighthearted than he had in weeks. "Coffee's all I need today. With Blane doing the chores, I didn't have a chance to work up much of an appetite. Besides, I want to get to the church early and look over my notes before the service. If I don't get a move on, I won't have time." He gave her another quick peck on the cheek and headed back toward his room.

"Don't forget to take a razor to those whiskers," Ma called after him.

Anthony stopped and turned to face her. "I thought I might let them grow." He rubbed his hand over his jaw, already irritated with the itchy growth.

"I see."

At the look of understanding on Ma's face, Anthony's ears heated up. He knew better than to think a man's outward appearance mattered. These people were more than willing to give him a chance in the beginning, knowing full well how young he was. A beard and mustache were not going to make a difference if he couldn't somehow find a way to reach their hearts.

Clearing his throat, he turned without another word and strode to his room to dress in his Sunday suit and get rid of those irritating whiskers.

CHAPTER 3

Tarah closed the door after the last of her students filed into the schoolhouse following their lunch break.

Only two more hours, she consoled herself as she walked to her desk. Then she could go home and nurse her pounding headache — depending on how long it took Luke to write his punishment sentences for the day.

Yesterday she had made him write, "I will not place bent nails in any other student's chair." One hundred times. Today he would have to write, "I will not place frogs in any other student's lunch pail." Why he would want to do such things was beyond Tarah. If he wanted to spend his afternoons writing sentences, that was his choice, even if it meant she had to stay after school, as well.

Rapping on the table with her ruler, she called the school to attention. She released a frustrated breath as the clamor continued. The three McAlester girls screamed and ducked when a slate pencil flew across the room. Tarah rapped again — harder. "Take your seats immediately!"

"Ow! Let go!" Emily's cry of pain echoed off the walls.

"Jeremiah Daniels," Tarah called above the chaos. "Turn loose of Emily's braid and go stand in the corner."

The boy glared back at her, defiance sparking in his eyes.

The room grew quiet as the children watched the exchange. They waited, as did Tarah, to see what Jeremiah would do.

Please, God. Make him obey me.

She met his gaze evenly. "In the corner . . . Now!"

He scowled but slowly slipped from his seat and made his way to the corner.

With a relieved sigh, Tarah turned to the other students. "The rest of you pull out your readers and just . . . be quiet for a few minutes."

Wearily she sank into her chair. *Crunch!*

A sense of dread hovered over Tarah like a thick black cloud about to burst. Pressing her palms to her desk, she pushed herself to a standing position, pinning Luke to his wooden bench with her gaze. She gathered a slow breath and glanced at her chair. Fury rose inside her at the sight of messy egg remains. She twisted and found the rest of the shell and yoke stuck to the backside of her new calico dress.

The children snickered until she glared at the room, hands on her hips. That was it!

"Luke!" she bellowed.

After almost four weeks of absolute chaos, he had finally driven her to her breaking point. Standing in the corner didn't bother Luke, writing sentences certainly didn't deter him, and Tarah had decided telling Pa and Ma was no longer an option. She had to show them she could handle things on her own. And right now, she was going to do just that.

"March yourself up here this instant, young man."

"What'd I do?"

His look of innocence only infuriated her more.

Snatching up her ruler from the desk, she faced him. "You know very well what you did, and it's not going to happen again."

Tarah gathered in another breath for courage. She had never believed in corporal punishment in the schoolroom, but now she understood why other teachers used the ruler on their students. Sometimes other forms of punishment just did not work. "Hold out your hand."

"But, Tarah, I didn't —"

"When we are in school, you will address me as 'Miss St. John' like the other children," she said through gritted teeth. "Now hold out your hand."

"Miss St. John?"

Tarah turned at the sound of Josie's quavering voice. The little girl sat white-faced in her seat, worry clouding her eyes.

Tarah gave her a dismissive wave. Of course Josie didn't want Luke to be whipped. More often than not, they were partners in crime. Well, that was too bad. This time Tarah was getting the upper hand. She'd show them all they couldn't get away with terrorizing her anymore.

"But, Miss St. John —"

"Sit still, Josie. I'll be with you in a moment," she snapped.

Turning her gaze back to her brother, Tarah almost gasped at the tears in his eyes. She pushed away the compassion threatening to melt her resolve and raised her brow. "Well?"

Slowly he gave her his palm.

Tarah flinched as the ruler came down with a resounding *smack*.

"Please, Miss St. John." Josie slipped from her seat and made her way to the front.

"Wh–what is it?" Tarah whispered, unable

to pull her gaze from the look of betrayal on Luke's face.

"It wasn't Luke."

"What do you mean?" Panic tore across Tarah's heart.

"I — I put the egg on your seat. Luke didn't know anything about it. Honest." The little girl slowly inched her hand forward, palm up. She squeezed her eyes shut while she awaited her punishment.

All the strength drained from Tarah, and the ruler dropped to the desk with a clatter.

"Luke, I —"

"May I go back to my seat, *Miss St. John?*" Despite his stormy gaze, his bottom lip quivered.

Tarah nodded. With great effort, she faced her class. The wide, questioning eyes and even fearful expressions on some of the younger children's faces were more than she could bear. "School is dismissed for the day," she croaked. "Tell your parents I–I'm not feeling well."

Somehow she managed to stand on wobbly legs until all of her students but Luke silently gathered their belongings and left the school. He walked to the blackboard. Folding his arms, he stared daggers through her.

"What do I write today?"

Filled with remorse, Tarah couldn't blame him for the belligerence in his stance and tone. "N–never mind, Luke. Go on home, and tell Ma I'll be along later."

Silently he walked to his desk and grabbed his things.

"Luke," Tarah said, tears nearly choking her.

"What?"

"I'm sorry I didn't give you a chance to explain."

Luke shrugged. "Didn't bother me none." He slipped outside before she could say more.

Unmindful of the mess, Tarah sank back into her seat. Folding her arms atop the desk, she pressed her forehead onto the backs of her hands. Sobs shook her body.

It's just too hard, Lord. I can't do it.

"I can't give ya any more credit until ya pay what ya owe. And that's all there is to it."

Anthony tried to pretend indifference to the exchange between the ragged stranger and the storekeeper but found himself unable to look away.

"Please, Tucker," the man begged. "You know I got them two youngsters to feed. I'll pay ya soon as I sell off a pig."

Anthony surveyed the man's shabby, thin

clothing and greasy hair. He figured it must have taken a lot of courage for a fellow to swallow his pride and ask for help. Compassion rose up within him.

What would it hurt to extend the man credit for a little while? He glanced at the storekeeper, and his heart sank. Tucker was having none of it. "Look, John, ya promised the same thing last month an' the month b'fore. I just can't do it."

Unable to endure the look of misery on the man's face, Anthony stepped up beside him. "Look, Tucker, just put his order on my account."

The creases on Tucker's face deepened. "I don't think that's such a good idea, Preacher," he said, warning thick in his voice.

"You let me worry about that," Anthony replied. He extended his hand to the ragged stranger.

A nearly toothless grin split the man's face as he reached out a filthy hand and gripped Anthony's. "I'm obliged to you, sir. An' dontcha worry none; I'll pay ya every last cent, soon as I sell that pig."

"I'm sure you will. I'm Reverend Greene." Anthony felt his chest swell at the admission. "I haven't seen you before. Just move into the area?"

"Name's Jenkins. Got two fine youngsters at home waitin' fer me."

"We'd love to see you and your family in church on Sunday."

The man shuffled and scratched at his long, matted beard. "Well now, Preacher, we ain't much for religion an' all that. But seein' as how yer bein' so generous an' all . . ."

"Oh no. There are no strings attached to this. But I hope you and your family will come to church anyway. We'd love to have you."

"Here's your order, John." Tucker grudgingly pushed a box filled with supplies across the counter. Anthony glanced inside and frowned at the pouch of tobacco and two bottles of Healy's Magic Elixir lying on top.

Jenkins nearly leaped at the box, grabbed it up, and headed for the door. "Much obliged, Preacher," he mumbled before the clanging bell announced his departure.

Tucker shook his head as Anthony handed him a list of his own. "That was a mistake, Preacher. Jenkins is a no-account if I ever seen one." He moved away from the counter to fill the order. "And I seen plenty of his kind in my day, I can tell ya."

"Took a lot of guts to ask for credit after

you turned him down."

"Guts." Tucker snorted and grunted as he lifted a twenty-five-pound bag of flour from the shelf. "He was in here yesterday and the day b'fore and the day b'fore that."

"That so?" Anthony asked, a twinge of unease creeping into his stomach. "I've never seen him around here. Where's he from?"

A shrug lifted Tucker's thin shoulders. "Don't know and don't care. But he owes me seventeen dollars. And he ain't gettin' another thing from this store 'til he pays up."

"Do you happen to know where his homestead is?"

"He ain't got one. Al Garner found the whole slovenly family squattin' in the old soddy he built back in '55 when he first moved into the area. Would have thrown them out, but for the little girl and crippled boy."

"It was the Christian thing for Al to do. I'm sure the Lord is pleased with his generosity."

Tucker set the last of Anthony's supplies in a large crate and snorted again. "It was a fool thing to do if ya ask me. He'll never get rid of that no-account. Already feeds his family most of the time."

Anthony tried to contain his irritation, but Tucker's coldhearted remarks were beginning to go against his grain. "Well, you know the Lord did say if a man asks for your shirt, give him your coat, too."

Leaning an elbow against the counter, Tucker pointed a finger at Anthony, his eyes glittering with determination. "Let me give ya a little advice, Preacher. Get ready for a cold winter, 'cause if ya let Jenkins hornswoggle ya, you'll be goin' without a coat b'fore the week's out. And most likely your boots, too."

"Maybe so," Anthony shot back. "But I can't just turn my back on a family in need."

"Don't that Bible ya like to quote also say something about a man having to work or he don't eat?"

"Well . . ."

Tucker gave a curt nod. "Thought so." As though it settled the matter, he grabbed the account book and began to tally.

"Make sure you add Jenkins's supplies to my account, Tuck."

"That's what I'm doin' right now."

"Good." Anthony clapped his hat on his head and picked up the heavy crate. "And I hope to see you in church this Sunday. We've missed you the last couple of weeks."

"Been busy, Preacher. Now dontcha forget

I warned ya about Jenkins."

"I won't. But I think you'll be surprised when he pays you your money and proves you wrong." At least he sure hoped the man made good on his promise. Otherwise Anthony would look like the fool Tucker obviously thought him to be.

Straining under the weight of the crate filled with supplies, Anthony stepped from Tucker's Mercantile into the bright autumn day.

"Why, Anthony, how lovely to see you."

He nearly dropped the wooden box as Louisa Thomas came out of nowhere and clutched his arm.

"Hello, Louisa. Fine afternoon we're having, isn't it?" He smiled politely.

"Just heavenly. I love autumn weather the best." She beamed up at him and tightened her grip. "My, you are strong, aren't you?"

He could hold his own, but those supplies were getting awfully heavy. If she didn't turn him loose pretty soon, he'd be forced to ask her to step aside.

Apparently oblivious to his plight, Louisa continued to smile enchantingly at him. He had to admit the attention was flattering, and he didn't want to be rude, but . . .

"Excuse me, Louisa." His voice sounded strained to his own ears.

53

"Oh, now don't tell me you haven't the time for a little chat." She pursed her lips into a pretty pout. "I've hardly seen you at all since you got back to town."

"I know, but . . ."

Anthony felt his grip loosen on the crate and feared any second the entire load would fall and land on the lady's toes.

"I am absolutely not going to let you go unless you promise to have a picnic with me after church on Sunday."

He had planned to ask Tarah to accompany him on an outing Sunday, but given the circumstances, perhaps he should accept Louisa's invitation instead.

"Okay. That sounds fine," he said with a grunt.

"Wonderful. It'll give us a chance to catch up on the last two years." Thankfully she turned loose of his arm to clap with delight. "I'll make you a delectable lunch. And a chocolate cake for old time's sake. How does that sound?"

"Sounds pretty good. I'll be seeing you."

Anthony heaved the crate into his wagon and paused to rest for a moment. When he turned, he came face-to-face with Louisa.

Startled, he reached out and grasped her arms to keep from knocking her over.

"Why, Anthony," she said breathlessly,

leaning in closer. Her lips pursed as though she expected him to kiss her right there in the street. Abruptly he let her go and retreated a step.

Disappointment clouded her green eyes, but she recovered quickly as the sound of children's laughter diverted her attention to the schoolyard across the road.

Anthony glanced over Louisa's shoulder and watched the children calling good-bye to one another and heading off in different directions.

"That's strange," he mused. "School shouldn't be out for a couple of hours yet. I wonder if something's wrong."

"Oh, who knows?" Louisa said with a wave of her hand. "Tarah probably decided to give them the rest of the day off."

"I wonder why, though. It isn't like Tarah to be irresponsible."

Sidling up next to him, Louisa once again curled her fingers around his arm. "Well, she did run off with that awful Johnny Cooper a couple of years ago."

Now that was an uncalled-for recollection. Anthony felt himself tense. Downright catty, if he had to give it a name.

For some reason, he felt the need to defend Tarah's honor, and he resented being put in the position to do so. Still, he couldn't let the unkind statement go unchallenged.

"If memory serves correctly, Tarah didn't exactly run off with her pa's foreman; he kidnapped her *and* her stepmother." He wanted to be perfectly clear he didn't believe Tarah had been defiled in any way — if that's what Louisa was insinuating. And he had an uncomfortable feeling she might be suggesting that very thing.

A tinge of pink colored Louisa's cheeks, then she lifted her chin. "Well, she was *going* to run off with him until she found out he only wanted to get his hands on her pa's money. At least that's what she told Myra Rhoades."

Louisa snorted in a not-so-flattering manner. "And you know Myra couldn't keep a secret to save her life."

Feeling the need to put an end to the conversation that bordered dangerously on gossip, Anthony gave her a cheery grin. "Well, praise God, Dell and Doc Simpson caught up with them in time to keep them all safe."

A smile curved Louisa's lips. "Oh, I agree completely. I just shudder to think of Cassidy's babies being born out in the snow and cold. God surely was with them that night."

Anthony searched her wide, innocent eyes, looking for evidence of guile. He found nothing. Perhaps he had misjudged her. Most folks had a penchant for gossip more than they should. But that didn't mean Louisa intended anything unkind in her remarks.

"But you must think I'm awful," she said, mist forming in her eyes. "I should never have mentioned poor Tarah's unfortunate incident."

Patting her hand, Anthony gave her a reassuring smile. "Of course I don't think you're awful. But perhaps we should leave those things in the past, as I'm sure Tarah would like to do."

She beamed up at him. "Of course she would like to put it all behind her, poor girl. And I certainly don't blame her. I know I'd just die if anyone knew such horrid things about me."

Unease crept through Anthony's gut. Was she being catty again? At her look of complete innocence, he felt a niggling of guilt. If he was going to be a preacher, he'd have to learn not to judge people so quickly.

Two boys strolled past, heading for the mercantile. Anthony frowned as he overheard their conversation.

"Boy, she gave it to Luke good, didn't she?"

"Well, I don't like her. She's too bossy. Besides, Luke didn't even do anything this time."

"Oh dear," Louisa said, shaking her head, a troubled frown furrowing her brow. "It would appear Tarah's having difficulty with her students."

"I'm going over there to see if there's a problem."

She made no move to let go of his arm.

Frustrated, Anthony searched for a way to get her to let go without being rude. "Louisa, will you tell Mr. Tucker I'm leaving my team in front of the mercantile while I check on Tarah? I'll be back to get it in a few minutes."

Her eyes narrowed but brightened again in an instant. "Of course I will, Anthony. You're so sweet to be concerned. But then, I guess that's why you're the preacher." She squeezed his arm before letting go. "I'll tell Mr. Tucker. Now don't you forget about our picnic on Sunday. I'll have everything ready so we can leave directly after your wonderful preaching."

Releasing a breath, he strode toward the school. Concern crept over him. Josie and Luke sat on the steps. At the sober expressions marring each face, Anthony started to worry.

"But we have to do *something.* It wasn't fair!" he heard Jo declare, indignation thick in her voice. "We're not going to let her get away with —"

"What's going on?" Anthony asked.

Josie's head shot up, worry flickering in her blue eyes. "Miss St. John isn't feeling well, so she dismissed us early," she said. Her gaze darted to her boots.

"Josie, look at me," he said sternly.

Reluctantly she inched her chin upward until he caught her guilty gaze.

"Now what happened? Is Miss St. John really sick?"

Her slim shoulders lifted. "That's what she said."

"Luke?"

"I guess so."

Something wasn't right.

"You stay here and wait for me," he instructed his niece. "I'll drive you home as soon as I'm sure your teacher's all right. I mean it, Jo. Stay put. Do you hear me?"

"Yes, Uncle Anthony."

Anthony opened the door. Alarm clenched his heart at the sight of Tarah, head on her desk, sobbing like a child. He closed the distance between them in a few long strides and crouched beside her.

She didn't look up as he reached forward and drew her close. Slumping against him, she rested her head on his shoulder and cried all the more.

Anthony searched for words of comfort, but finding none, he remained silent. Stroking her hair while she cried, he couldn't help but think how right this felt. As though she belonged in his arms. *Lord, are You trying to tell me something?*

He drew in a breath, the lavender scent of her hair filling his senses.

"D–do you have a handkerchief?" Tarah pulled away and looked at him, her eyes luminous from the tears.

"Huh?"

"Something I can wipe my nose with?"

Rats! He didn't. He gave her an apologetic smile. "I'm sorry."

She scowled.

Should he offer her his sleeve?

Just as he was about to suggest it, he had a better idea. He pulled his arm from around her shoulders and stood. He took out his pocketknife, then untucked a corner of his shirt. While Tarah watched with a furrowed brow, he swiped at the cloth until a piece came off in his hand.

Once again, tears pooled in her eyes as

she accepted the makeshift handkerchief and blew her nose. "Thank you. That was sweet."

Anthony's heart soared as he stared into her red, splotchy face. "What's all this about?"

"I'm a bad teacher, Anthony." She hiccupped.

"I'm sure that's not true, Tarah. Toby's learning to read so well. He loves school."

"But the discipline," Tarah countered. Her shoulders shook as she began to sob again.

"Come on, now," Anthony said gently, crouching beside her once more. "It can't be that bad." He reached for her, then pulled back as she shot from her chair.

"It can't, huh?" Her eyes flashed as she glared down at him. "Do you know what I just did?"

Anthony gaped at the quick switch from sorrow to anger.

"I just took my ruler and smacked Luke on the hand for something Josie did." She gave him a satisfied nod. "You see, I can tell by the look on your face how shocked you are."

Rising from his crouched position, Anthony hesitated a moment, not sure he wanted to ask the question begging to be voiced. He drew a breath. "What exactly did Jo do?"

She spun around. "Just look at the back of my dress!"

Anthony groaned. So that's why the girl was so eager to gather the eggs this morning. "But why did you punish Luke if Jo put the egg in your chair?"

All the steam seemed to leave the slender young woman, and she dropped back into her chair. "I — I just assumed it was Luke. He's been so horrid ever since I paid him to be good."

"You paid?"

She nodded, and her eyes filled up again. "He didn't have the money to pay for Josie's ribbons — you remember the ones he inked that first day of school — so I offered to give it to him if he would just stop instigating trouble. I — I thought it sounded like a good solution."

Several questions circled in Anthony's head as he tried to make sense of what he was hearing.

"And he didn't keep his end of the bargain?"

"Oh yes. For as long as it took to pay for the ribbons. Then he was worse than any child I've ever seen, except maybe —" She stopped midsentence.

"Josie," Anthony supplied.

"Yes." Her voice was barely audible as she averted her gaze.

"Do you mind my asking why you didn't just tell your folks? Seems like your pa could deal with Luke with one trip to the woodshed."

"I didn't want them to think I couldn't handle it," she said. "Besides, I don't want Pa and Ma to worry. They have enough to think about with the new baby coming."

"Are there problems with Cassidy's, er, condition?"

"No. But my ma died having Jack, so Pa worries."

Now that was exactly the kind of thing Dell should have come to Anthony about. As preacher, he could have prayed with him and quoted the scriptures about God not wanting His people to be anxious. When would these people take him seriously? He blew out a frustrated breath.

Tarah glanced up, questions written on her face.

Anthony shook his head, inwardly berating himself for thinking about his own problems at a time like this. "I'll take care of Jo," he said firmly, "so you won't have to worry about her causing any more problems."

A shrug lifted Tarah's shoulders. "It

doesn't matter, because I'm quitting. Louisa Thomas wanted the position when they gave it to me. Well, she can have it." Tarah stood. "Thank you for being so kind. I'm sorry about your shirt."

"The shirt doesn't matter, Tarah." He placed a hand on her arm. "Things will straighten out. Don't quit just yet."

"I can't face the students after what I did today."

Compassion filled Anthony at her self-loathing. "Listen, how about if I teach your students for a couple of days while you pull yourself together?"

Tarah's full lips parted as she drew in a breath. "I can't ask you to do that! Your ma needs you at home. Besides, won't the town council object?"

"I've been planning to pass on more responsibility to my brothers anyway. Blane's old enough to take care of things now. And I'll be there to help out at night. As for the town council, I'll talk to Mr. Tucker and Mr. Gordon before I leave town. And you can talk to your pa since he's head of the council."

Once again, her eyes filled. "I — I just don't know, Anthony. The look on Luke's face . . ." Tears rolled down her cheeks, and suddenly she was in his arms again.

"Shh . . ." He held her to him, stroked her hair, and felt as though he would never breathe again.

The door swung open, and Anthony caught Josie's stormy gaze. Behind her, Luke still sat on the step. Jo placed her hands on her small hips and stomped her foot. "Are we ever going home?"

Tarah disengaged herself from his arms and gathered her books from her desk. "I — I have to go. Ma will worry when the children get home early."

"Do you want me to come tomorrow?"

After a moment's hesitation, Tarah nodded. "Thank you, Anthony."

Her lovely gaze captured his for a moment. She gave him a tremulous smile and pressed her fingers lightly to his arm. Before he could recover from the shock of her touch, she walked past Josie and left the little school without a backward glance. Luke stood and followed.

As he watched her walk away, Anthony prayed a silent prayer of peace for Tarah.

"Are we leaving now?" Jo's impatient voice drew him back to face a reproving stare.

Anger flashed through Anthony. "Yes. Right now. You and I have some talking to do, young lady."

"I'll say. Me and Luke saw you cozying

up to Miss Thomas over by the mercantile." She waved both hands in the air to emphasize her words. "I bet the whole town saw you. And now me and Luke catch you hugging Miss St. John." She gave him a disapproving frown. "Just how many girls are you courting, Uncle Anthony?"

Chapter 4

Tarah waited just inside her bedroom door until she heard Jack, Luke, and Emily head off to school, then she made her way into the front room.

"Tawah!" Hope ran to greet her. Grabbing Tarah around the legs, she hugged tightly.

Tarah snatched the little girl up in her arms and kissed her plump face. Drawing the child close, she pressed her cheek against her little sister's silky head and breathed in her sweet baby smell. A niggling of guilt inched through her stomach. She hadn't spent much time with the twins lately and hadn't even realized until this moment how much she'd missed them.

Not to be outdone, Will clutched at Tarah's skirts. "Me, too."

Laughter bubbled within Tarah. "You two are getting too big for me to hold you both." She knelt on the wooden floor and gathered them into her lap. "What are you playing with?"

Will wiggled free and held up a wooden train engine. "Twain."

"Why, where did you get that?"

"Sam."

"Oh, how nice. What sound does a train make?"

Will's "woo-woos" brought a giggle to Tarah's lips.

Hope scrambled from Tarah's lap and jerked the toy from Will's hand.

"Mine!" the little boy hollered.

"Hope, sweetie," Tarah said, "the train belongs to Will. Give it back."

A scowl darkened the otherwise angelic face. "No!" She snatched the toy back as Will made a grab for it. Clutching the engine tightly to her chest, she ran toward the kitchen, Will close on her heels.

Releasing a sigh, Tarah stood and followed.

The kitchen door opened and Cassidy appeared, holding a mug in her hands. Hope flung herself against Cassidy's skirts. "Ma!"

Relieved to have the situation out of her hands, Tarah plopped into a wooden chair and watched the drama unfold.

"What on earth is going on?" With Hope pressed firmly against her legs, Cassidy inched her way to the table and deposited the steaming cup she held.

"My twain!" Will shouted.

"Was Hope playing with it first?" She looked to Tarah for the answer.

Shaking her head, Tarah gave her a wry grin.

Cassidy bent at the waist until she met Hope eye to eye. "Honey, you can't take away a toy your brother is playing with. That's not nice. Give it back and tell him you're sorry."

With quivering lips, Hope shoved the engine into Will's outstretched hands.

"And tell him you're sorry," Cassidy prodded.

"Sowwy." Eyeing the train as though she would like very much to snatch it back, the toddler didn't look a bit sorry. Tarah ducked her head to hide her grin.

"There's a good girl." Cassidy pressed a kiss to each dark, curly head. "Now go play nicely together for a little while." She dropped into her chair and grinned at Tarah. "Good morning," she said, reaching for her cup.

Tarah knew her stepmother took a few moments for herself each morning. After the uproar and confusion associated with getting everyone out of the house for the day, she needed to relax before cleaning up the breakfast mess.

Cassidy didn't look a bit frazzled by the twins' antics. Her jade-colored eyes twinkled as she glanced at Tarah over the rim of her cup. "I figured you were hiding out until the kids left for school. With those two acting up this morning, you probably wish you'd stayed in bed." She smiled again. "Are you ready for breakfast?"

"I'll get it," Tarah replied, smiling back at her stepmother. "Enjoy your coffee. As a matter of fact, I'll do the cleanup for you, too."

"Why, thank you. I remember a time when I had to practically force you to lift a finger."

Tarah groaned. "I was something else in those days, wasn't I? I don't know why you put up with me."

"When you're part of a family, you don't have a choice. Why don't you go get your breakfast, and we'll have a nice little chat. It seems like ages since we've spent any time together."

"Good idea." Tarah hurried into the kitchen and grabbed her plate from beneath a towel at the back of the stove. She made her way back to the table and settled, once more, into her chair across from Cassidy.

"But you did things so well," she said,

picking up the conversation where they'd left off. "Luke and Sam and I, and even Granny, were so horrid to you in the beginning, but you still managed to take care of us and love us in spite of it. I don't know how you did it."

"I certainly made my share of mistakes, though, didn't I?" Cassidy said wryly. "For instance, I should have told your pa about your relationship with Johnny Cooper from the moment I knew about it. It might have saved you a lot of heartache, not to mention the danger my silence put you in."

Tarah shuddered. She didn't want to think about that awful night with Johnny. Still, Cassidy didn't deserve the blame. "That wasn't your fault. I promised you I wouldn't see him anymore. If I had kept my word, he never would have kidnapped us."

"Anyway, those days are behind us, praise the Lord." Cassidy sipped her coffee, then set the cup down. "And look at you now, all grown up and teaching school. I'm so proud of you."

Tarah gave a short laugh and jerked a thumb toward the twins, at last playing peacefully in front of the fireplace. "I can't even get those two to obey me. You should see the mayhem in my classroom." With a gasp, she realized her admission and glanced

71

up from her plate to meet Cassidy's sympathetic gaze.

"Want to talk about it?"

"Oh, I don't know. I'm just not a very good teacher. The children won't obey me. It's a wonder they learn anything at all with all the disruptions from Luke and Jo."

"Luke, eh? Is he still causing trouble in school?" Cassidy shook her head.

"More than ever." Now that she had begun, the words poured from Tarah like a fast-running stream. "I put him in the corner, and all he does is make faces behind my back. The other children think he's just hilarious." Tarah pushed the food around on her plate. With her stomach clenched, she knew she couldn't eat a bite.

"Miss Nelson once told me that standing Luke in the corner was just another way for him to cause trouble," Cassidy said. "Sounds like he hasn't changed much."

Placing a hand to her forehead, Tarah groaned. "I'm so tired of staying thirty minutes after school just so he can write sentences for his punishment. He writes them as slowly as he can just to get under my skin. I've been trying to think of another method of punishment for him, so yesterday —"

Tarah stopped, not sure she wanted to

admit to her error.

"What happened that was so bad you had to take a day off?"

Tears stung Tarah's eyes as the memory of the sound of the ruler on Luke's hand came back as vividly as though he were standing before her. She poured out the entire story, omitting nothing, including Anthony's visit afterward. By the time she had blurted the whole wretched tale, tears streamed down Tarah's face.

Cassidy reached out and covered one of Tarah's hands. The comfort of the warm touch made her cry all the more.

"I just can't do it anymore," she sobbed. "I had such high hopes of being a wonderful teacher. I never thought the children would hate me."

"Oh, Tarah, don't be so hard on yourself. Luke is a special case." Cassidy handed her a napkin to dry her tears. "He might act up a little worse for his sister than he would for another teacher, but he definitely caused trouble for Miss Nelson, too. I know it's difficult, but he has to understand that your relationship at school isn't the same as here at home."

Grateful for the support, Tarah voiced the question she had been contemplating since the day before. "Do you think I should talk to Pa about it?"

Cassidy gave a reflective frown. "You could. Your pa would certainly take care of it, I suppose. And I doubt Luke would cause more trouble in school."

"That would be a relief."

"I'm sure." Cassidy nodded. "But he would probably make up for the trouble he can't cause you at school by taking it out on you here at home."

"Oh, Ma," Tarah groaned, hating her whiny tone of voice. "I just don't know what to do."

"Tarah," Cassidy said, "Luke needs to know who's boss. And at school, that just happens to be his sister. I don't argue the fact that you should have gotten the full explanation before you unjustly punished Luke, but don't be so hard on yourself."

"I can't help it. I'm at my wit's end in dealing with him and Josie Raney."

"Luke's ornery; there's no denying that," Cassidy said. "But he has a good heart, and he loves you. Maybe you should try reasoning with him."

"My twain! Ma!" Will's cry cut off Tarah's retort.

Lips twitching in amusement, Cassidy stood. "I'd better find those two something to do before the 'twain' ends up broken."

She pushed in her chair, her gaze searching Tarah's face. "It was kind of Anthony to offer to teach today."

Feeling the heat rise to her cheeks, Tarah swallowed hard and nodded.

As if sensing Tarah's reluctance to discuss Anthony, Cassidy gathered a breath and blew it out. "So what do you have planned for your day off?"

Grateful that Cassidy didn't seem inclined to press the matter of Anthony further, Tarah found her voice.

"I thought I'd go for a ride. Down to the river maybe, then into town to see if Mr. Tucker has any mail for us. I was hoping to ride Abby since Lady is about to foal. Is that all right with you?"

"Of course. It'll do her some good. Your pa won't let me near the horse until the baby comes. Make sure you pack a lunch in case you decide to stay out for a while. And, Tarah," she said, a look of hesitancy clouding her eyes.

"Go ahead," Tarah urged.

"If you've prayed about this and it doesn't seem as though God is answering, perhaps you should ask Him if there is a lesson He wants you to learn from your reaction to Luke's behavior."

"My reaction?" Tarah's defenses rose. Her

reaction was just as it should be. Luke was the one out of hand, and he was the one who needed to be taught a lesson!

"I don't want to hurt you, and you know I'm not excusing Luke, but often the way we react to pressure teaches us more about our own hearts than we would ever learn if things always worked out smoothly for us." Cassidy regarded Tarah with a sympathetic smile. "Just a thought."

Striding into the living area, she clapped her hands together. "All right, you two, give me that train, and let's go find some wildflowers to decorate the table."

Anxious to go for her ride, Tarah grabbed her plate and Cassidy's cup from the table and set about tackling the dishes.

A strong wind blew across the prairie as Tarah gave Abby her head and let the horse run through the tall grass. Breathing deeply of the cool October air, Tarah felt the heavy weight lift from her shoulders.

The confinement of the schoolhouse seemed far away, and she had almost definitely decided to turn in her resignation. Only the thought of Pa's disappointment troubled her about her near decision. And he would surely be disappointed.

Feeling the weight descending upon her

once more, Tarah urged Abby on, faster, toward the river. Only when the horse's labored breathing matched Tarah's did she slow down and allow the animal to walk the rest of the way. At the riverbank, she dismounted and led Abby to the water.

Tarah looked out over the river, wishing for the peace usually brought about by the gentle rush of waves lapping against the bank.

So many questions were plaguing her mind. Should she continue teaching? Did she even want to? And if she did, what should she do about Luke and Josie?

Cassidy's words rushed back, bringing a troubling introspection she would rather do without. *Lord, are You trying to teach me something? If so, what? How on earth can I learn anything from Luke and Jo's meanness?*

"Howdy."

Tarah jumped and whirled around, nearly dropping Abby's reins.

A child of no more than seven or eight years stood staring at Tarah, wide brown eyes sizing her up as though she were a cow at an auction. At second glance, Tarah realized the child was a girl, though she wore filthy trousers with holes in both knees and a threadbare button-down shirt that Tarah supposed had once been white. Long, matted hair, which could have been either brown or dark auburn, hung around the girl's shoulders.

"Cain't you talk?"

Tarah found her tongue. "Of course I can talk."

"How come you didn't say nothin', then? When I said 'howdy,' that is." She reached out a grubby hand and patted Abby's rump.

Tarah's cheeks flamed at her own rudeness. "I'm sorry. I was just surprised to see anyone out here today. I thought I'd have the place all to myself."

The little girl glanced up wordlessly and shrugged. Turning, she sauntered away.

"Wait. Where are you going?"

"Thought ya wanted to be alone," she called over her shoulder.

Oh, honestly. Tarah followed, catching up easily. "I didn't say I wanted to be alone. I'm just surprised to find anyone else out here. I'm sorry I made you feel unwelcome."

Stopping, the little girl eyed her. She gave a shrug and nodded. "It's okay. I'm used to no one wantin' me around. Don't bother me. I just don't stay where I ain't wanted. That's all."

Tarah's heart wrenched with the thought that any child could feel unwanted. "Actually, I wouldn't mind some company. Want to come back to the river and talk to me for a while?"

"I reckon," the little girl replied, heading back toward the river without waiting for Tarah. "Ain't got nothin' better to do."

"What's your name?" Tarah asked, falling into step beside her.

"Laney."

"That's pretty. I've never heard it before."

"Short for Elaine." Laney scowled. "But don't call me Elaine. I hate it."

"You have my word." Tarah's lips twitched with amusement.

"So what's yer name?"

"Miss St. John."

"You ain't got a first name?"

"You can call me Tarah, I suppose."

"Nice to meet ya, Tarah." The girl extended her grimy right hand in greeting.

Swallowing hard, Tarah shook Laney's hand, trying with difficulty to hide her distaste.

They settled onto the bank of the river. Downwind from the child, Tarah fought hard not to pinch her nose to keep the stench away. If this girl had ever had a bath, it certainly hadn't been in the recent past.

"Laney, I haven't seen you around before, and Harper's a small township. Are your folks new to the area?"

79

"I dunno. We been here awhile, I guess."
Laney jerked her thumb behind them. "We
live over thataway."

"But that's Al Garner's land. He owns all
the property between here and town."

"That's right. Pa's a squatter," she said
matter-of-factly. "Mr. Garner knows about
it, though. Said we could live in the old
soddy, long as we don't wreck the place."

"I see." Feeling uncomfortable with her
own prying, Tarah tried to think of something else to talk about.

"Usually," Laney continued as though the
topic of conversation didn't bother her one
bit, "we get thrown off a place 'fore we can
settle in real good. We been here longer than
anyplace in as long as I can remember."

"Why haven't your ma and pa sent you to
school?"

"What fer? I can read good enough, if the
words are little. Ain't got no books anyways,
'cept Ma's old Bible, and who wants to read
that? And I can do sums up to the hundreds.
I figure that's all a body really needs to
know. 'Sides, ain't got no ma, just a pa and
Ben."

"You don't have a ma?" The words left
Tarah before she could rein them in. That
certainly explained Laney's appearance.
What kind of a pa left a child to fend for

herself with no thought to education or cleanliness?

"Nope. She died when I was a young'un. Cholera or somethin', I guess. Pa never talks about it. Ben remembers her, but I don't."

"I'm sorry, honey." Tarah wanted to reach out to the child, to draw her close and give her a woman's touch, but she couldn't quite push through the revulsion. The way Laney scratched her head, she more than likely had lice in her hair. Tarah shuddered at the thought and inched away just a little, praying diligently the child wouldn't notice.

"It don't matter none anyways." A shrug lifted Laney's bony shoulders, and her chin jerked up. "A person cain't miss someone they never knew."

"I miss my mother every day," Tarah said softly.

"Yer ma's dead, too?" Laney regarded her through narrowed eyes.

"Yes. She died when I was a little older than you."

"Too bad." She tossed a twig into the water and watched the river claim it.

"I have a wonderful stepmother, though," Tarah said.

"Yer pa must be a fine man. Ain't a woman alive dumb enough to marry my pa."

"Laney! What a thing to say!"

"It's the truth. And I don't care who hears me say it." With a stubborn set of her jaw, she tossed another stick into the river.

"I'm sure your pa's a fine man." Tarah nearly choked on the words. She had already drawn her own conclusion of the unknown man, and apparently the child held the same opinion.

"No, he ain't, and if you knew 'im, you wouldn't even claim such a fool thing."

Stung, Tarah drew a breath. "Well, no matter what sort of man he is, the Bible instructs children to honor their parents."

"I don't hold to no religion, Tarah. So I don't much care what the Bible has to say about the subject."

Stifling a gasp at the irreverence, Tarah searched for a way to reach Laney, but the girl jumped to her feet. "Look, lady, I don't need no lectures. I'm near twelve years old, and soon as I can, I'm gettin' away from that old drunk."

So the man was not only slovenly; he indulged in liquor. That explained a lot. The girl's age surprised Tarah. She was no taller than seven-year-old Jack and quite a bit skinnier. Surveying Laney critically, Tarah decided the child was half-starved.

"Wait, Laney. Don't go yet. It's a bit early for lunch, but I'm getting a little hungry.

Do you want to share with me?"

Laney's eyes grew stormy, her lips twisting into a sneer. "I don't need yer charity."

"Oh, honestly." Tarah stood and made her way to Abby. "I packed more food than I can possibly eat." Knowing she'd be away from the house most of the day, Cassidy had insisted Tarah pack enough food for an army. Tarah had thought it silly at the time, but now she was glad for Cassidy's forethought. "If someone doesn't help me eat it, most of this will go to waste." Tarah pulled a blanket from the saddlebag and spread it on the ground.

"Well . . ." Laney eyed the leftover chicken and thick slices of bread Tarah set on the blanket.

"You might want to go to the river and wash your hands," Tarah suggested.

"What fer?"

"Because they're dirty. You shouldn't eat with dirty hands."

"That so?" She shrugged. "Don't guess it'd hurt nothin' to swish 'em around a little."

"I'm sure it wouldn't," Tarah drawled.

Laney returned a moment later, wiping her wet hands on the filthy trousers. Tarah cringed. It hardly did any good for her to wash. The dirt was apparently ground in so deep, a good scrubbing would be necessary to get her hands clean. Laney didn't seem to notice and ate with abandon, barely swallowing one bite before taking another.

Nibbling on a slice of bread, Tarah watched the girl down three pieces of chicken and two slices of bread. At Tarah's insistence, she accepted the only piece of apple pie left over from supper the night before.

Rubbing her stomach, Laney emitted a loud belch, then groaned. "Don't think I've ever had such good food. You folks eat like that all the time?"

"My ma is a wonderful cook."

"Thought ya said yer ma was dead," Laney challenged.

"She is. I told you my pa remarried."

"Oh." Laney stood. "I best get back to the house 'fore Pa wakes up and starts hollerin'."

Tarah stood and faced the girl. "Laney, I teach in town. Will you consider coming to school?"

"Yer the teacher?" Her brown eyes narrowed suspiciously.

"That's right."

"Then why ain't ya at school?"

Heat rushed to Tarah's face. "I took the day off."

"Never heard of a teacher playing hooky b'fore."

Tarah laughed. "Someone is looking after my class for me. I didn't leave them to their own devices. So how about it? Think you might like to come?"

"And yer the teacher, huh?"

"That's right. I'd love to have you there."

After a moment's hesitation, she shrugged. "Well, seein' as how ya shared yer food with me . . ." She inclined her head. "Guess it wouldn't hurt nothin' to try it out. But if I don't like it, ya cain't make me stay."

Tarah's heart soared. A giddy feeling enveloped her, and she grinned. "Thank you, Laney. I hope you'll like school."

Hungrily Laney eyed the two remaining pieces of chicken and the bread still left on the blanket.

Tarah cleared her throat and stooped to wrap the leftovers in a napkin. "Would you mind taking this home with you? I'm heading into town and would rather not have it in my saddlebag. The smell will attract every dog in Harper."

Light flickered in the girl's eyes. "Guess I could. Ben'll probably like it." Her lips turned down bitterly. "If Pa don't grab it away from him."

"Is Ben your brother?"

"Yep. He don't walk so good."

"Why not?"

"Horse stepped on him a couple years back."

The story grew more heartbreaking with each new chapter, and pity clutched at Tarah's heart for the unknown boy. "Maybe you could slip him the food when your pa's not looking."

Laney grinned. "Think I'll do that, Teacher. You goin' to school tomorra?"

Suddenly Tarah wanted nothing more than to return to her classroom and teach. Luke or no Luke, she was determined to be a success. If she made a difference in only one child's life, it would be worth the effort. "Yes, I am. I really am, Laney."

Giving her a curious glance, the girl clutched the bundle of food to her chest and inclined her head once more. "Reckon I'll prob'ly see ya then."

"I'll look forward to it."

Wordlessly Laney turned and wandered away as suddenly as she had appeared.

With renewed resolve, Tarah turned back to the blanket. She shook it out, then stuffed it back into the saddlebag. Casting one last glance across the wide-open prairie, she watched as Laney's retreating form grew smaller.

If she made a difference in only one child's life . . .

CHAPTER 5

Releasing a self-satisfied breath, Anthony leaned back in his chair. The day was going pretty well so far. No disruptions. The children attended their studies diligently with only an occasional whisper here and there. Apparently after all the commotion of the day before, they didn't want to push their substitute teacher. Anthony was grateful, but he hoped the compliance would last should Tarah decide to return to her classroom.

Feeling a rumble in the pit of his stomach, he pulled out his pocket watch and noted the time. "All right, children," he said. "Put away your books and stand to your feet. It's time for lunch."

The room rustled with the sounds of books closing, desktops opening then dropping shut, and the children scooting from their seats.

"Who wants to say the blessing before we

get our lunches out?"

A shuffling of feet answered, and not one pair of eyes met his gaze. "Oh, come now. No volunteers? I suppose I could pick someone."

He glanced around at the room of suddenly very subdued students. "Jo?"

"Oh, Uncle Anthony. Pick someone else!"

"Come up here," he replied firmly. "You can certainly say a prayer over lunch."

With eyes sparking, she stomped to the front, stopping when she reached the desk.

Soft laughter filled the room.

"That's enough, class," Anthony said. "Go ahead, Jo."

Blue eyes flashed as she jutted out her chin. "Bow your heads, folks," she said. "It's time to pray."

The little scamp could do without the sarcasm and dramatics, Anthony thought. But at least she didn't out and out refuse to obey.

"Our most gracious heavenly Father," she began, her voice deepening. "We thank Thee for Thy most holy presence."

Indignation rose up in Anthony at the obvious imitation of his own prayers on Sunday mornings. The children snickered. He raised his head and opened one eye to look at his niece, then widened his scope to take in the rest of the children. Every eye was open and watching Josie.

She waved her arm with a dramatic flare. "Have mercy on this group of sinners, Lord. They don't know how close they are to the pit of hell."

Now he'd never prayed that in the service. She must have heard his private prayers. *The little eavesdropper!*

"Josie Raney! That's quite enough. Go back to your seat."

With a toss of her thick blond braids, she headed for her desk, a smug grin playing at the corners of her lips.

"Bow your heads," he commanded. After a quick blessing over the food, he dismissed the class for lunch, his own appetite suddenly gone.

While the children ate lunch and had recess, Anthony pulled out a large hollowed-out sandstone he had placed in the desk drawer that morning before the children arrived for school. Inside the stone, he had packed clay made from the soft earth at the bank of the river. He pushed at the mixture to be sure it was still soft, then nodded.

As a preacher, he would be remiss in his duties if he didn't give the children a lesson for their souls as well as for their minds. Knowing how they fidgeted during his

Sunday sermons, he had prayed for a creative way to get his message across in a manner children could understand. An idea — too much to be coincidence, he thought — had come to him in the night. Filled with anticipation, he had awakened extra early to go to the river and collect the materials needed to carry out the message.

By the time he rang the bell to end recess, he was ready to begin. When the children were settled and quiet, he decided to let them in on the change in routine.

"We're dispensing with lessons for the rest of the day —"

A cheer rose up from the students.

"But you're not leaving early. We're going to have a little Bible lesson." He picked up his Bible from the desktop.

Walking around to the front of the desk, he eyed the children, noting the look of dread on each face. Heat crept up the back of his neck.

Help me, Lord. Let these children understand the message You've given me to share with them.

He leaned against the desk and opened his well-worn Bible to Jeremiah eighteen and began to read. "Then the word of the Lord came to me, saying, 'O house of Israel, cannot I do with you as this potter?' saith the Lord. 'Behold, as the clay is in the potter's hand, so are ye in mine hand, O house of Israel.' "

Anthony closed the Bible, set it back down on the desk behind him, and looked out over the schoolroom. "Anyone know what that means?"

He received a roomful of blank stares in response.

A sigh escaped his lips as he held up the sandstone for the students' inspection.

"Who would like to try to shape something out of this rock?"

Jeremiah Daniels's hand shot up.

"Jeremiah? You'd like to try?"

"Nah, Preacher. You lived in the city too long. You can't make nothing out of an old rock."

"You don't think so? What would you say if I were to tell you that some folks' hearts are just like this stone?"

Encouraged by the children's now-rapt attention, Anthony forged ahead. "Some hearts are hardened because they don't believe in Jesus. Others believe in Jesus and then allow sin into their hearts until slowly they become hardened again."

A quick scan of the children's faces spurred Anthony to move to the object lesson before he lost them. He pulled out his pocketknife, then sat on the desk. "Anyone who wants to can come up here and gather around the desk. I want to show you something."

The seats emptied as the students made their way to the front, curiosity written upon each face.

"Lord, forgive me of my sins." Slowly Anthony chipped off a piece of the sandstone with his knife. "Lord, I want to live for You." Again he chipped away at the stone. The children watched in silence. *Father, help them to understand.*

"Lord, I want Jesus to be my Savior." Another piece of stone slipped away onto the sod floor.

He stopped when the stone was half the original size. "Any questions so far?"

Jeremiah Daniels raised his hand again. "Yes?"

"Preacher, you been sinning?"

Anthony felt the wind *whoosh* out of him.

"Oh, Jeremiah. Everyone sins. Even preachers. This stone represents a human heart without God. When we ask for forgiveness, the stone begins to fall away, like so . . ." He chipped away a few more pieces. "You see, it's difficult to do what's right when there is so much sin in our hearts."

He continued to break away the pieces

around the clay. "Every sin, every act of disobedience, makes the stone bigger, and it's difficult for God to shape our hearts into what He wants us to be. But when we repent, the stone begins to fall away. Does that make sense?"

"You mean like when I tell a lie to get out of a thrashing, I get rocks in my heart?"

"Figuratively speaking," Anthony drawled.

"Or doing mean things to the teacher?" Emily asked, cutting her gaze first to Luke, then to Josie. Luke's ears turned red. He scowled at his sister.

Anthony nodded. "The Bible says we are to respect those in authority over us. And we shouldn't do mean things to anyone, regardless of who they are. Each sinful act makes it that much easier to do it again unless we repent."

"You know, that's true," Jeremiah spoke up. "First time I stole a sourball from the mercantile, my heart started beatin' real fast. But I didn't get caught, so I figured I'd do it again. And it was a lot easier after that. Think some of that stone built up so my heart wouldn't beat so fast, Preacher?"

Emily spoke before Anthony could answer. "Stealing's just plain wrong, Jeremiah Daniels," she declared, hands on hips. "You probably have more rocks in your heart than all of the rest of us put together, except maybe Luke, since he's so mean to Tarah."

"When was the last time you had a sourball?" Jeremiah asked hotly.

Emily tossed her orange braids. "Just last night. My pa brought us some from Tucker's. But he didn't steal them," she said pointedly. "He bought them fair and square."

"Well, no one's bought me any since *my* pa died last year." He glanced up at Anthony with eyes that begged him to understand. "Sometimes my mouth just itches for the taste of them ol' sourballs. But Ma says there's no money for such things. Guess it's still wrong, huh?"

With great effort, Anthony swallowed past the lump in his throat. He reached out and smoothed the boy's hair, then quickly pulled his hand away so as not to embarrass him. "I'm afraid so, son," he said, finding his voice with difficulty. "Sometimes doing what's right is hard. But it makes a boy into a real man with godly character in the long run."

Anthony decided this was as good a time as any to drive home the point of the lesson. He chipped at the last of the stone to reveal the clay within.

Glancing at Jeremiah's contrite face, he

extended his hand toward the boy. "You said I couldn't make anything out of the rock, but what about this? Think you could mold this into something?"

A shrug lifted Jeremiah's thin shoulders. "Sure." He took the ball of clay.

The children remained silent as the mound slowly took shape in Jeremiah's hands.

"It looks just like a turtle!" Emily said, admiration glowing in her green eyes.

"Is that what you wanted to make, Jeremiah?"

" 'Course. Or I'd have made somethin' else."

"What if you had wanted to make a turtle out of the clay but couldn't get to it because of the stone around it?"

"I'd do what you did and chip off the stone."

"Well, what if you didn't have anything to chip it off with?"

"Then I don't guess I could've done it."

"Exactly." Anthony's spirit soared. "God wants to form our hearts into what He wants us to be, but if we are hardened against His hands, He can't do it. But the knife here," he said, "is just like telling God you're sorry. It chips off pieces of stone until all that's left is the clay. Then God can begin to mold us just like He wants to." He scanned the small circle of children around him. "Remember the scripture I read when we started?"

Their blank faces confirmed they had already forgotten.

" 'As the clay is in the potter's hand, so are ye in mine hand.' Remember?"

Every head nodded.

"I want you to think about whether your heart is soft and easy to work with or hard like stone."

The door opened, allowing sunlight to filter into the room. Anthony's heart lurched at the sight of Tarah, standing with a confused frown on her face.

"Hello, Miss St. John," he said with a grin. "We were just finishing up a Bible lesson. Think anyone would object if we let them out a bit early today?"

"I suppose that would be all right."

The children cheered and scrambled to their desks to grab their belongings.

Jeremiah hung back. "You know, Preacher," he said, a reflective frown scrunching his brow. "If you preached like this on Sunday, a lot more folks would come and listen to you."

Stung, Anthony didn't know what to say, but he felt like the boy expected a thanks.

"Well, thank you, Jeremiah, I'll keep that in mind."

The boy nodded and turned to walk to his desk.

"Jeremiah, do you want to take this?" Anthony held out the turtle.

Flushing with pleasure, Jeremiah walked quickly to the desk and took his creation. "Thanks, Preacher!" Then he was off in a flash.

With a grin, Anthony glanced up at Tarah, who had made her way to the front amid the scramble of children.

She eyed the floor in front of her desk critically. "What in the world did you do, Anthony?"

Tarah scowled, awaiting Anthony's explanation.

"We've been having an object lesson."

"An object lesson?" She glanced into his grinning face.

Anthony nodded. "You don't think I could pass up a chance to preach to a captive audience, do you?"

Tarah tried to hide her horror. *Those poor children!* Then, feeling guilty for her thoughts, she plastered a smile onto her face and swallowed hard. "How did it go?"

Anthony shifted off the desk with a shrug. "Started out a little slow, but I think they got what I was trying to show them." Kneeling down, he began to pick up the pieces of stone from the floor. "We talked about how sin makes our hearts stony, but repentance chips away at the stone until all that's left is a heart easily molded into what God desires us to be. That's what all this mess is about. I wanted to show them instead of just preaching at them."

Tarah's stomach jumped. Was her heart as hard as this stone where Luke was concerned?

Shaking off the thought, Tarah bent down to help Anthony clean up. Her hand brushed against his, sending her heart racing as they reached for the same piece of stone.

Raising his head, Anthony searched her face. Tarah felt heat rush to her cheeks.

"How was your day off?" he asked in a soft, velvety voice.

Tarah stood and brushed at imaginary specks of dirt on her dress, trying to compose herself. "Nice," she said. "I appreciate you filling in for me."

Anthony stood, as well, and moved to the open window. "Should I plan to come in tomorrow?" He tossed out the pieces of stone and pulled the shutters closed. Brushing his hands together, he strode back to the desk.

"No. I met a girl down by the river today who said she might come to school tomorrow. I need to be here just in case she shows up."

"A girl?"

Tarah nodded. "Did you know there is a family of squatters living on Mr. Garner's land?"

Anthony nodded. "I met Mr. Jenkins in the mercantile yesterday, as a matter of fact. But that was the first I'd heard of them. The little girl you met is his daughter?"

"She didn't tell me her last name, but I assume so." Tarah walked around the desk and sank into her chair. "Oh, Anthony, it's enough to break your heart. Laney was filthy and wore torn, thin clothing. Not even girls' clothing, but boys' trousers and a button-down shirt."

With a nod, Anthony hoisted himself back onto the desktop and let his gaze roam across Tarah's face. "Her pa wasn't clean either, and his clothes looked like they might fall apart any moment."

"Children shouldn't have to live that way. Isn't there something we can do for them?"

A shrug lifted Anthony's broad shoulders. "A man has his pride, I guess. I'm not sure how much help Mr. Jenkins would accept. Of course, he did let me . . ."

Tarah waited for him to continue. When he looked away, she frowned. "He let you what?"

"It doesn't matter. Let's just say I believe he would probably be grateful for anything we could do for him."

Though her curiosity was piqued, Tarah realized he wouldn't elaborate, so she decided not to make him uncomfortable by asking questions. Instead, she pursed her lips reflectively. She shifted her gaze to Anthony to find him studying her mouth. Catching her bottom lip between her teeth, she cleared her throat.

Anthony's ears reddened, and he averted his gaze, suddenly intent on studying his hands.

"What do you think we should do?" Tarah asked after taking a moment to compose herself. She couldn't help the excitement flooding her. Was Anthony finally beginning to notice her? Oh, she hoped so!

"I guess basic necessities should come first."

"Huh?" Mentally kicking herself for being swept away on dreams of Anthony courting her, Tarah stared dumbly, waiting for him to repeat himself.

"For the Jenkinses. Basic necessities."

"Oh, of course." *Honestly!* "With winter

right around the corner, I suppose they will need clothing first off."

"Yes."

"Do you think we should ask for donations? Maybe Mr. Tucker . . ."

Anthony shook his head. "No. Not Tucker."

"Why not?"

"Jenkins owes him money for supplies over the last couple of months."

"Judging from some things Laney said about him, I guess that doesn't surprise me." Resting her elbow on the desk, Tarah tucked her chin into her palm. "Anthony?"

"Yes?" His soft gaze captured hers, and again Tarah lost the capacity to voice her question. An uncomfortable but short-lived silence hung between them as Tarah recovered her voice. "I was just wondering if you've ever known a man given to drink. Laney told me her pa doesn't work because he's drunk all the time."

Indignation clouded Anthony's eyes. "Is that right? I didn't know that, or I wouldn't have . . ."

Again he didn't elaborate.

"Do you think the folks around here would be willing to help such a man?" Tarah asked.

"I don't know." A frown creased his brow.

"Mr. Tucker quoted me the scripture about a man not eating if he won't work. He doesn't seem inclined to do much to help. If he's spoken to any of the other folks about it . . . I just don't know."

"But what about the children? Laney and her brother — Ben, I believe she called him. The boy's crippled."

Compassion moved over Anthony's features, endearing him to Tarah all the more. "Don't fret about it," he said, giving her a gentle smile. "I'll ask around and see what I can do. But even if only you and I help, the family will have more than they would have had otherwise. We can't let the children do without or become sick in the cold weather just because their pa won't lift a finger to help himself."

"Thank you, Anthony. I think this is the right thing to do. I'm so glad you agree and are willing to help me."

Leaning over, he reached out and traced a line from her cheekbone to chin. "I guess I'd do just about anything for you, Tarah."

A gasp escaped Tarah's throat. "Y–you would?"

The door opened suddenly, and he moved away, leaving Tarah to wonder if it had been a dream.

"Why, Anthony, you're still here, aren't

you?" Louisa's singsong voice echoed through the schoolroom as she sashayed to the front of the room.

A look of guilt flickered in Anthony's eyes, and he hopped from the desk. Tarah's temper flared. From the tight, possessive grip of Louisa's hand around Anthony's arm, it was apparent she held some claim on him.

Humiliation started at the top of Tarah's head and drifted to her toes. How dare he trifle with her affections! She would not be fancy's fool again where Anthony Greene was concerned. Shooting to her feet, Tarah gave Louisa her brightest smile. "How lovely to see you. I was just leaving." Turning to Anthony, she was hard-pressed to keep a civil tongue in her head. "Will you close the door on your way out?"

Anthony held a cornered-animal look in his eyes. "Tarah —"

"Oh, Anthony," Louisa said, a tone of reprimand in her voice that Tarah didn't quite believe. "Where are your manners?" She cut her gaze to Tarah, a beautiful smile curving her thin, rosy lips. "Of course we'll close the door when we leave."

"Thank you."

Tarah squared her shoulders and made her way down the aisle to the door.

"Tell me all about your day of teaching school," she heard Louisa ask as she shut the door firmly behind her.

Stomping to Abby, Tarah fought to keep her tears at bay. She unwound the reins from the hitching post in front of the schoolhouse and climbed into the saddle.

Why did Anthony prefer Louisa? He always had. She had been a fool to allow herself dreams of becoming his wife. Jerking her chin, Tarah turned Abby toward home and gave her a nudge.

"Tarah, wait!"

The sound of Anthony's voice brought her about. She pulled Abby to a stop, her traitorous heart racing like a runaway train. Watching as he jogged to catch her, Tarah willed her pulse to return to normal and arranged her face in what she hoped was only a look of mild interest.

"What's wrong?" she asked.

"I'm sorry about . . ."

Tarah followed his gaze to the schoolhouse, where Louisa stood, hands on her hips, lips twisted into a scowl.

"Think nothing of it, Anthony." Tarah attempted a short, teasing laugh. "Far be it from me to interfere with your courting."

"It's not like that —"

"Was that all you needed?"

Anthony swiped his hand through his thick, sandy blond hair, then cupped the back of his neck. "Actually, I thought maybe you would like to ride out to the Jenkins place with me — unless you needed to get home right away. I'd like to meet the children and maybe talk to Jenkins a bit."

"I can ride out there with you."

Flashing her a heart-stopping grin, Anthony nodded. "Good. Let me grab the team from the livery and we can tether your horse to the back."

Tarah watched him walk away, admiring the dignity with which he carried himself. A niggling of regret passed through her. Why did Anthony have to be interested in the likes of Louisa Thomas?

"I hope you had a restful day off." Louisa's irritating voice broke through Tarah's musings. Reluctantly she pulled her gaze from Anthony's retreating form to face the young woman.

"Thank you, Louisa. I did. I look forward to coming back tomorrow."

"I'm sure that's a relief to poor Anthony. It isn't as though he doesn't have enough to do without taking on your duties, as well."

Wishing very much she could think of a crushing retort, Tarah swallowed her anger and met Louisa's deceptively innocent gaze with a smile she was far from feeling.

"I'm sure he will be glad to get back to his own duties tomorrow. But I was certainly grateful he *offered* to help me out today."

"Yes, children can be a challenge at times." Louisa's smile didn't reach her eyes.

"Yes, they surely can. Of course, any job is a challenge, wouldn't you think? Sometimes I wish I had just stayed home to help my ma." Tarah released an exaggerated sigh. "But when the town council asked me to teach, I couldn't very well refuse, could I?"

Tarah felt a guilty sense of glee as Louisa's face colored at the reminder that she had been passed over for the teaching position in favor of Tarah.

"I suppose it must be *nice* to have your pa on the town council," Louisa countered, lifting a delicate brow in challenge.

Temper flaring, Tarah dropped the reins and put her hands on her hips. "Now wait just a minute. That had nothing to do with —"

"All set to go?"

Intent on putting Louisa in her place, Tarah hadn't even noticed Anthony pull up in the wagon. She dismounted and brushed past Louisa. "I'm ready," she muttered.

Anthony hopped down and grabbed Abby's reins from Tarah's shaking hands.

Without waiting for his help, Tarah climbed into the seat while he tied Abby to the back of the wagon.

"Where are you two off to?" Louisa asked in ill-feigned nonchalance.

"We're going to check on a new family in the area. Tarah is concerned for the children, and we're going to see what we can do to help."

"Oh, Anthony," Louisa said breathlessly. "What a wonderful idea. I'd love to help. May I come along?"

If Tarah could have spit to remove the bad taste in her mouth at Louisa's tactics, she would have done so with relish. *Say no, Anthony,* she silently pleaded.

"I don't see why not."

"Wonderful. I just love children. I want a house full of them someday." Louisa held on to Anthony's hand as she climbed in through the driver's side. "Don't you, Anthony?"

Tarah nearly gasped at the woman's brazenness. Did Louisa have no sense of propriety?

Anthony flushed and settled in beside Louisa. "I suppose I'd like children someday. When the right woman comes along."

Knowing that wasn't exactly the response Louisa was looking for, Tarah turned away to hide her grin.

With a sigh, she looked to the distant horizon and sent another prayer toward heaven. *How many lessons must I be forced to learn at a time?* Dealing with her attitude about Luke was one thing, but Louisa Thomas was another circumstance entirely. Years of animosity couldn't just disappear overnight. And the way Louisa was clinging to Anthony made Tarah want to smack the smug expression from her face. Her nails bit into her palms as she tightened her fists in an attempt to gain control over her raging emotions.

The wagon lurched as a wheel dipped into a rut in the road. Louisa took the opportunity to snuggle in closer to Anthony.

Drawing a long, steadying breath, Tarah wished for all she was worth that she had never agreed to go along. From the raised brows and friendly waves of passersby, she was sure they made quite a spectacle: Anthony, Louisa Thomas, and her.

CHAPTER 6

"Oh my! This is the most disgraceful thing I've ever laid my eyes on. And the smell! Who on earth would live in such a place?"

The look of revulsion on Louisa's face, as well as the tone of her voice, sent a tremor of irritation through Anthony. This family needed help, not judgment. Admittedly Jenkins was slovenly and a drunk, to boot. But the children weren't at fault for their pa's sins. And after all, Laney and Ben were the reasons he and Tarah felt the need to offer assistance in the first place.

He slid his gaze to Tarah's. Her face held a similar look of revulsion, but when she turned toward him, Anthony observed tears pooling in her eyes. He knew her thoughts were on the children being forced to live in such squalor. Wishing very much that he could pull her close and comfort her, Anthony did all he knew to do and gave her what he hoped to be a reassuring smile.

When he had maneuvered the wagon as close to the soddy as he could amid the clutter strewn about the yard, he tugged on the reins, pulling the horses to a stop. He hopped from the wagon and reached out his hand to assist Louisa.

"I just can't believe people live this way!" she declared, pressing a lacy handkerchief to her nose.

"It is a hard thing to take in," he admitted. "But you might want to keep your voice down a little so we don't hurt anyone's feelings."

Sidestepping a broken wagon wheel, Anthony walked around to help Tarah down. She sat unmoving, staring at the run-down soddy. Anthony followed her gaze. Wagon parts littered the yard, along with a broken washtub and dozens of empty liquor bottles. Anthony couldn't stop the anger from building inside him. How could a man claim to be a pa and allow his children to live in such filth? The way the man had let Garner's place run down was nothing short of shameful.

A wooden door lay on the ground outside the opening to the soddy, and a thin blanket hung in tatters across the doorframe. At the window, a shutter swung loosely by one hinge. At the edge of the house stood a thin, swaybacked mare, pitifully trying to pull up the dead grass from the ground.

"Come on," Anthony said softly. "Let's go see what we can do for those children." Rather than offering a hand as he had to Louisa, Anthony instinctively opened his arms.

Turning sorrowful eyes upon him, Tarah stood and allowed him to lift her from the wagon. Anthony swallowed hard, wishing they were alone so he could ask her permission to court her. In the back of his mind, he knew this wasn't the proper time or place, but at the moment, his rapidly beating heart remained at odds with his head.

His senses cleared as Tarah placed her hands on his arms, still encircling her small waist, and gave them a gentle push. Instantly he released her.

With a furrowed brow, Louisa hurried to stand next to Anthony. "This is all just so . . . horrid." She held tightly to his arm, her long fingernails digging in as though she feared for her very life.

Staring at the devastation, guilt pricked Anthony. This was no place for either young woman. Already his skin crawled at the thought of what they might find inside the soddy.

"Hello?" he called as they reached the

doorway. "Anyone home?"

The rusty barrel of a shotgun poked through a hole in the blanket. Anthony stepped back suddenly, pulling Louisa with him. He narrowly missed knocking against Tarah and reached out to steady her.

"Get on outta here, mister," a child's voice commanded. "We got a right to this place. Ain't no one but Mr. Garner gonna throw us out."

"Laney? It's Tarah. Can we come in?"

The blanket was pulled back, and the dirtiest little urchin Anthony had ever seen emerged from the soddy. Her face split into a wide grin at the sight of Tarah. "Whatcha doin' here, Teacher? I told ya I'd be at yer school tomorra."

Tarah stepped forward. "I wanted you to meet a friend of mine."

Anthony disentangled himself from Louisa and stepped forward.

Laney eyed him warily, then gave his proffered hand a firm shake. "You her beau?" she asked, jerking her head toward Tarah.

"He certainly is not, young man." Louisa pushed forward and reclaimed her place at Anthony's side.

"Sor–ry, lady." Laney's eyes flashed as she looked Louisa up and down. "And I ain't no boy. I'm a girl, same as you. Only I'd rather be tarred and feathered than wear a getup like you got on." She squinted and peered closer. "And my pa says only loose women paint their faces. And if there's one thing my pa knows about, it's loose women. Though I wouldn't hold to what he has to say about nothin' else."

A gasp escaped Louisa's lips. Anthony stood in stunned silence, cutting his gaze to Tarah. Her face glowed red, and a hand covered her mouth as she tried hard to hide her amusement.

Louisa held herself up primly. "I do *not* paint my face, young *lady,*" she replied hotly. "And I will thank you to keep a civil tongue in your mouth when addressing an adult."

"I'll talk any way I want to, lady. And you are so wearin' paint."

"I am not!"

"Want me to prove it?" Laney shot back, stretching her hand toward Louisa's face.

Louisa recoiled. Anthony caught Tarah's gaze and silently pleaded with her to intervene. Nearly choked with suppressed mirth, Tarah obviously couldn't speak for fear of doubling over and howling with laughter.

Louisa seemed to be managing pretty well anyway, so Anthony left her to her own defense. "Don't you dare put your hands on me! I have never seen such an ill-mannered, filthy child in my life."

"I don't recollect askin' your opinion, lady. And who invited you anyways?"

She had a point there. Anthony strongly regretted allowing Louisa to accompany him. But when that young woman put her mind to something, she had a way of getting what she wanted. Although he couldn't excuse the child's rudeness, neither could he help but feel that Louisa was getting a little of what she deserved from the sharp-tongued girl.

Louisa dropped her death grip on Anthony's arm and placed her hands on her hips. Indignantly she looked from Tarah to Anthony. "Are you two going to just stand there and allow this child to insult me?"

To Anthony's relief, Tarah finally found her voice. "I believe you have equally insulted one another, and you *both*," she said pointedly, lifting a delicate brow as she observed Louisa, "deserve an apology."

Anthony grimaced, anticipating Louisa's reaction.

"I certainly will *not* apologize to that . . . that . . . creature!"

Yep, just as he thought.

"I ain't 'pologizin' to no hoity-toity lady with her nose ten feet in the air, neither. And ain't no one makin' me do nothin' I don't wanna do."

Louisa stamped her foot on the ground. "I will not stand here and be insulted another moment. Let's go."

With that, she swung around and stomped toward the wagon. Stopping halfway to her destination, she looked back. "Well, Anthony? Are you coming?"

"We'll be along in a little while." Completely disgusted with Louisa's behavior, Anthony was in no mood to give in to her whim. "I think you're right, though. It might be best if you wait in the wagon."

Louisa's jaw dropped, and her face grew pinker than usual. Without a word, she spun around and stomped back to the wagon.

"Whew!" Laney said. "That's some girl you got there, mister."

"Just for the record," Anthony said, "she's not my girl."

Laney shrugged. "Two bits says she gets her claws in you and walks you down the aisle, one way or another, if you get my meanin'. Pa says Ma roped him into marryin' up with her 'cause she was gonna have Ben, and he regretted it ever since. So you just watch yerself, mister."

Heat crept up the back of Anthony's neck and seared the tips of his ears.

Tarah cleared her throat, her own face

tinged with pink. "Laney, honey, Reverend Greene is the town preacher."

Laney scowled. "We don't hold to no religion, Preacher. I done told Tarah I ain't got much use for the Bible and such."

Still trying to recover from the child's crude statement, Anthony nodded. "Your pa mentioned something about that when I met him at the mercantile yesterday."

With a shake of her head, Laney released a heavy sigh. "I don't know why that Tucker's dumb enough to keep givin' my pa credit. He ain't never gonna get his money."

Taken aback by the disrespectful words, Anthony frowned. "Sure he will, after your pa sells the pig."

Laney chortled. "Preacher, I hate to tell ya this, but if we had a pig, I'da shot it for food a long time ago. Pa sold off every animal we owned when he took to drinkin' a few years back. He'd sell that old nag over there, too, if anyone would buy her."

Remembering the words Mr. Tucker had spoken about being hornswoggled, Anthony felt like a fool. Mr. Jenkins had lied and cheated his way into his good graces.

A twinge of guilt pricked Anthony at the harsh feelings rising up inside, because in truth, he had offered his help to Jenkins. The man hadn't asked him for anything.

Not that he hadn't taken advantage of Anthony's good nature — then lied to him about paying him back.

"And if any man will sue thee at the law, and take away thy coat, let him have thy cloak also."

The desire to give the scoundrel a sound thrashing was stronger than ever, and Anthony struggled to contain his anger and focus on the children, who didn't deserve to be punished for their pa's underhanded ways.

"Is your pa around?"

"Passed out cold," Laney said, her lips twisting into a sneer. "Probably won't wake up 'til near dark. Why'd you want to talk to him anyways?"

"I have something to discuss with him."

Laney nodded, curiosity written on her dirty face. "Best time to talk to my pa is between the time he wakes up and when he starts drinkin' again. I figure ya have near two hours a day b'fore he's too drunk. You can come back later iffen ya want."

"Thank you, Laney," Tarah said. "Do you and Ben have anything to eat for supper?"

"Yeah, we got beans left over from last night, and Ben'll have that chicken I took off yer hands earlier."

Anthony pressed a hand to Tarah's shoulder. "We'd better get going."

She nodded her response. "I'll see you at school tomorrow, right?"

"Said I'd be there, didn't I?" Laney replied. "And one thing ya can count on, Tarah. I always keep *my* word." She emphasized "my" as though trying to assure Tarah — and maybe herself — that she was nothing like her pa, who apparently never kept his.

Tarah smiled. "All right, then. I'll see you at eight thirty sharp."

"I'll be there." Laney grinned, showing white teeth, a startling contrast to her smudged face.

"And, Laney," Tarah said hesitantly, "would you mind calling me 'Miss St. John' at school? All the other students call me that, and I wouldn't want them to think I'm allowing you special privileges."

Laney seemed to consider the request for a moment, then her bony shoulders lifted. "Don't see why not. Wouldn't want ya to have no trouble on accounta me."

Anthony smiled at the way Tarah had handled the situation. As they strode back to the wagon, he told her so.

An enticing spot of pink appeared on each cheek at the compliment. "I didn't suppose she would do it if I tried to tell her she had to."

"She's mighty determined not to be told what to do, isn't she?"

"Yes, but she's obviously had to fend for herself and her brother for a long time," Tarah said, rising to the child's defense. "It's no wonder she's so independent."

"True. Still," Anthony mused, "I'm concerned about her bitterness toward her pa. To be so bitter so young is a terrible thing."

"Well, that's no wonder either." Tarah's voice rose. "Honestly, Anthony. The man drinks away any pittance of money he can dig up and lives off the charity of others."

"No one is so far gone that the hand of God can't reach him, though."

Tarah stopped in her tracks and glared up at him. "Anthony Greene, don't you defend that monster to me. I'd like to reach out *my* hand with a nice big skillet and use it over his head! That might be the only way to knock some sense into him." Without waiting for a response, she stomped to the wagon, untied Abby, and mounted. "Goodbye, Anthony, Louisa. I can ride the rest of the way home alone." With that, she turned her horse and rode away in a cloud of dust.

Anthony watched her go. The image of the tiny young woman taking on a man like

Jenkins filled his mind, and he chuckled to himself. It would serve the old drunk right if Tarah went after him.

"Anthony, I really must be going home." Louisa's clipped voice broke through his thoughts.

"Coming." Still smiling to himself, Anthony climbed into the wagon and headed the horses toward town. "All set?"

With her back perfectly straight, Louisa jerked her chin and set her lips into a grim line. All signs she was more than a little put out with him.

Rather than feeling distressed by her anger, Anthony felt a sense of relief that she wouldn't be chattering the entire ride into town. Odd how all her ramblings and flighty ways had once appealed to him. Now they were nothing more than irritations. Especially when she grabbed his arm and exclaimed over his strength.

Even as the thought came to him, so, too, did the image of Tarah's wide, luminous eyes and full lips. His mind wrapped around the memory of her slight form in his arms, and the way she had taken a dirty little girl under her wing, determined to do whatever she could to see the child had a chance.

Lord, this is the kind of wife a preacher needs. Someone with a heart of compassion.

Of course, it probably wouldn't be a good idea for her to actually follow through with that skillet. Perhaps You could allow her the grace to extend her mercy to include the entire Jenkins family.

"You should just see the place, Pa." Tarah filled Abby's trough with hay and gave her a pat on the neck. "Mr. Jenkins has let it become so run-down I almost didn't recognize it. Remember how Mrs. Garner used to keep it up and plant flowers all around the house? She must be rolling over in her grave about now."

Pa nodded as they walked abreast of each other toward the barn door. He closed and latched the door behind them. Pulling Tarah close, Pa steered her toward the house. "I've heard he'll do about anything for a drink. He must be a lonely, miserable man."

"And deserves no less," Tarah shot back as the run-down soddy and Laney flashed through her mind.

A frown etched his brow. "That's a pretty harsh statement."

"If you could just see poor Laney, Pa. I get so angry just thinking about it."

"Your anger won't do that family a bit of good, Tarah. Only your prayers. Just remember, God's love and grace extend to everyone. Not just the people we think worthy."

"That's what Anthony said."

"He's right." He paused a minute, regarding her thoughtfully. "Is there anything I should know about you and this young preacher?"

Heat rushed to her cheeks, but she shook her head. "He's courting Louisa Thomas." How she wished she could give him another answer.

"You sure about that?"

"Yes. Why?"

He shrugged. "I don't know. I'm sure Louisa's a fine young woman, but she doesn't seem suited to a man like Anthony."

The words sent a strange sense of comfort to Tarah's aching heart. She agreed wholeheartedly with her pa. There was only one woman suited to Anthony, and that woman certainly was not Louisa Thomas.

Moving to the door, Pa gave her a wry grin. "I suppose a man's got to make his own decisions about women. But it'll be a heap easier on him if he makes the right one."

Tarah followed, fighting to hold back the tears clouding her eyes. "If Anthony Greene can't see what's right under his nose, then it serves him right if Louisa sinks her claws into him," she muttered.

Pa stopped before opening the front door. "I thought you might have feelings for him." He studied her face for a split second, then opened his arms wide.

She went to him willingly, taking comfort from the slow *thud* of his heart against her ear. "Oh, Pa. Even back in our school days I favored him. But for some reason, he never saw me that way. It has always been Louisa. When he came back, I hoped he might see me in a different light."

"He did offer to take your class today," Pa reminded her, gently stroking her hair.

"We've become . . . friends, I guess," she admitted.

"Nothing wrong with friendship."

Tarah sniffed. "But I want more than —" She stopped, aware she sounded like a spoiled child crying for a new toy.

Pa held her at arm's length and silently regarded her for a long moment, until at last Tarah felt ashamed and dropped her gaze. He cupped her chin and forced her head gently upward. "And if his friendship is all he has to offer you right now?"

With great effort, Tarah swallowed past the lump in her throat and lifted her shoulders. "Then I guess I'll have to accept it."

He smiled, his approval causing Tarah's heart to soar. "I'm proud of you, sweetheart.

But don't give up on him just yet. You never know what God has planned." He reached for the door, then turned back to her with a grin. "Cassidy and I are proof of that."

As promised, Laney stepped inside the schoolhouse at eight thirty sharp the next morning. The room buzzed as the children observed the newest student.

"Never seen so much dirt on one person in my life."

Horrified by Luke's outburst, Tarah pinned him with her gaze until his face reddened and he turned away. Tarah swallowed past her indignation and glanced at Laney, who now stood motionless midway up the aisle. Struggling to keep from pinching her own nose to stifle the odor coming from the girl, Tarah pasted a smile on her face. "I'm so glad you came."

"Said I would, didn't I? And I always keep my word." Laney eyed the other children nervously.

"Yeah, but does she ever take a bath? Pee—ew."

The room filled with twitters of laughter at Josie's loud whisper.

A flicker of hurt flashed in Laney's eyes but left as soon as it had appeared. She squared her bony shoulders and glared at Josie.

Tarah's emotions waffled between compassion for the girl and anger at the children's cruelty. They had no idea the kind of life Laney endured on a daily basis. If Tarah could have her way, she'd march each one of them to the woodshed and give them the switchings they deserved.

"Josie Raney," Tarah said hotly, feeling Laney's humiliation. "Go stand in that corner. Luke, go stand in the other one. I will not tolerate rude behavior in my classroom."

Laney's brows lifted. "Aw, Tar— Miss St. John. You ain't gotta do that on my account. I'm used to it. Anyways, I don't stay where I ain't wanted." She turned on her heel, headed back down the aisle toward the door, then stopped as Luke brushed past her on his way to the corner. Grabbing his arm, she brought him about to face her. She raised up on her tiptoes and got as close to his face as her tiny body allowed. "Fella," she said. "If I had a face full of freckles like you, I wouldn't be worryin' over a little dirt. Least I can wash mine off iffen I take a notion to."

Squaring her shoulders, she spun around and slipped through the door as quickly as she had come.

Luke's face glowed red as the children laughed at Laney's rude remark. A twinge of sympathy rose within Tarah at his embarrassment. Luke had always been self-conscious about his freckles, and she knew Laney's comment had hurt him.

"I'm sorry, Luke," she whispered as he walked past her.

Surprise lit his eyes. He regarded her briefly, then shrugged. "Didn't bother me none."

She knew he was lying but didn't press the issue. "It bothered me. No one deserves to be treated unkindly." A feeling of unease clenched her stomach as Louisa's annoying face flitted to her mind. Stubbornly she shook the image away. That was an entirely different matter.

Without responding to her comment, Luke turned his back and pressed his nose into the corner.

Tarah turned to the other children. "I'll be right back," she announced. "Take out your readers and keep quiet until I return."

Once outside, she scanned the area for Laney. Her heart raced as she spied the child headed toward the direction of the old soddy. "Laney, wait!" she called.

The little girl stopped and waited until

Tarah caught up to her.

With a sinking heart, Tarah observed the stony expression on her face.

"It ain't no use, Tarah. I told ya I weren't stayin' iffen I didn't like it."

"Oh, Laney. You didn't give it a chance."

Laney set her jaw firmly. "I don't stay where I ain't wanted. 'Sides, school's a waste of time anyhow."

"Honey, I'm sorry those children were rude to you." Tarah felt her shoulders slump in defeat. "Believe me, I know how you feel."

Laney's eyes narrowed. "They say you stink, too?" She frowned and, leaning in close to Tarah, drew a deep breath. "I ain't noticed nothin' like that. Fact is, you smell kinda sweet — like I 'magine my ma smelt 'fore she died."

"Thank you, Laney." Tarah's heart ached for the motherless child who had to live in such squalor. "Please come back to school."

"Them kids don't like me."

"They just don't know you yet, honey. After a while, they won't have any choice but to like you — just like I do."

A glimmer lit Laney's eyes. "You like me?"

"Of course I do. From the moment we spoke at the river yesterday, I knew you and I would be friends."

Eyeing her warily, Laney cocked her head

128

to one side. "You ain't just sayin' that so's I'll come back for some learnin'?"

"I promise." Wings of hope fluttered in Tarah's heart, and she prayed as hard as she had in her entire life. *Please, Lord. Change this little girl's heart.*

"Cain't do it," Laney said, shaking her head. "Those kids don't like my clothes nor my smell."

"Well, maybe you could take a bath and put on some different clothes," Tarah suggested hopefully.

Laney scowled. "Pa kicked a hole in the washtub and . . ." She glanced away. "This is all the clothes I got. Sorry, Tarah. Ya been real good to me, and I wish I could go back. But I just cain't. Not with them sayin' such things about me."

Tears stung Tarah's eyes. She couldn't blame the child for not wanting to endure further humiliation. "I understand, Laney. Really, I do. And I'm sorry the other children were so mean." Her voice trembled as she spoke.

Laney's eyes grew wide. "Y–ya really do like me, dontcha?"

Tarah nodded, unable to find her voice.

Laney flew into her arms, nearly knocking her over with the force of her little body. Before Tarah could react, the child squeezed her tightly around the middle, then darted away as fast as her scrawny legs would carry her.

Tears flowed unchecked down Tarah's face as she slowly made her way back to the schoolroom. She drew in a deep, steadying breath, swiped at her cheeks with her palms, and stepped inside. Expecting chaos, she sent up a prayer of thanks when she found her students exactly as she had left them.

Luke turned to face her as she walked toward her desk. For the first time in weeks, no belligerence or teasing marked his expression. Instead, he regarded her with serious eyes, conveying his apology, then he turned and stood motionless with his nose pressed to the wall.

CHAPTER 7

Tarah shut the schoolhouse door firmly behind her and headed for Tucker's Mercantile. After the fiasco with Laney that morning, the children were mercifully compliant the remainder of the day. But Tarah took only minimal joy in the fact that they learned their lessons well and offered no resistance. Her heart still ached for Laney.

After praying for direction all morning, an idea had come to her around lunchtime. With great effort, she instructed the children in their lessons the rest of the day, impatient for the time when she could dismiss the class.

She walked the short distance to the mercantile, eager to put her plan into action.

"Afternoon, Tarah," Mr. Tucker greeted her as the bell above the door signaled her arrival. "Glad you're here. Got some mail for you."

"For me?"

"Yep." Faded blue eyes twinkled as he handed her an envelope. "Ya got this from some fella over in Starling. Finally court-in'?"

Tarah felt her cheeks warm. "No, sir."

She glanced down to make sure the letter was rightfully addressed to her. Sure enough, her name was written plainly on the envelope: Miss Tarah St. John, Harper, Kansas.

There was no mistake. Her heart did a little jump at the return address: Mr. Clyde Halston, a rancher friend of Pa's from Starling, a small community twenty miles north of Harper. He had come through to buy a horse last summer. The day he arrived, the household was filled with excitement over learning Tarah had been hired to teach in Harper.

At the time, Mr. Halston had mentioned the possibility of Tarah coming to Starling to teach a three-month term in the spring, but she hadn't taken him seriously. Now she wondered if perhaps the town council had taken his suggestion to start a school after all.

"Gonna open it or stand there staring at it all day?" Mr. Tucker asked, leaning his elbows on the counter.

Waffling between the desire to open her letter and wanting to complete her business, Tarah opted to wait. Reading the letter would come later, away from Mr. Tucker's prying eyes. "I think I'll wait. I need to make a few purchases and get home to help with chores," she said, tucking the envelope into her bag.

Clearly disappointed by her decision, Mr. Tucker straightened up and glanced at her over his wire-rimmed spectacles. "Got a letter here for your pa, too." He handed it over. "Looks like it might be from your granny."

Tarah smiled as she read the return address. "Yes, it is."

"When's she comin' back, anyway?" Tucker cleared his throat and gave the letter a once-over. "Some folks been sayin' how they're missin' her."

With great effort, Tarah bit back the smile threatening her lips. She knew Mr. Tucker and Granny had a mutual affection for each other, but so far, neither had lowered their pride enough to admit it.

"I'm not sure, Mr. Tucker," she said. "Perhaps this letter contains that information. We'll all be so happy when she returns to us."

"Make sure ya let me know so I can pass the word along to the folks askin' about her, ya hear?"

"Yes, sir."

"Now what can I get for ya?"

"I need two pairs of boys' trousers. About my brother Jack's size. Do you carry those? And two new shirts, also."

"I got 'em. On that shelf over there."

Tarah thanked the storekeeper and headed in the direction he indicated.

Originally she had toyed with the idea of getting Laney into a dress but dismissed the thought as quickly as it had come. She had the feeling if she tried, the girl would balk and refuse to wear the feminine garment. Next she had thought of asking Ma for some of Luke's castoffs, usually given to Jack, but decided against that, as well. She doubted Laney had ever owned new clothing, and she wanted the child to have something new, something no one else had ever worn.

She rummaged through the shelves until she found two sturdy pairs of blue jeans that looked to be about Laney's size and two shirts — one blue and one brown. On impulse, she grabbed some suspenders, just in case she had misjudged the size. Walking back to the counter, she spied a rack of coats. She glanced at the price and drew in her breath, mentally calculating how much of her meager earnings she would need to part with to buy one.

Reluctantly she turned away, knowing she didn't have enough to pay for the clothes and a new coat for Laney. The shirts were warm enough to shield the child from the cool autumn air for now, but Tarah knew Kansas weather. One day could be hot as July, and all of a sudden, a blizzard could blow up out of nowhere. But there was nothing she could do about it for the time being. With one last glance at the rack of coats, she turned to Mr. Tucker and set the items on the counter. "This is all, I suppose."

"I hate to pass up a sale, but you sure you need those shirts?" Mr. Tucker asked. "Your ma was just in here a few days ago buying material and buttons for new shirts all around. I recollect her mentioning she needed enough to get all her men through the winter."

"Yes. She's busy sewing now," Tarah replied, not wanting to give him more information than necessary.

Mr. Tucker raised his bushy eyebrows and pursed his lips. "Sure ya want all that?"

"Yes, sir." She averted her gaze, feigning interest in a jar of sourballs on the counter.

"Okay, then. Should I put this on your

pa's account?"

Tarah turned back to the storekeeper. "Oh no. I'm paying cash."

A curious frown etched his brow as he tallied the items and gave her the total.

Tarah reached into her cloth bag and drew out the money. "Mr. Tucker, how much for that washtub hanging on the wall?"

"Now hold on. Just what are you up to, young lady? I know your pa didn't send you down here for these clothes and a washtub."

A sigh escaped her lips. "All right," she said. "These things are for a needy child. But please don't tell anyone."

"What needy child?"

"Please, Mr. Tucker. Don't ask. I'd rather not say."

"Humph." He eyed her suspiciously. "These for the Jenkins boy? I'm telling you, they'll never fit him. He's about the size of your brother Luke."

Tarah gasped. She'd forgotten all about Ben. She drew in her lip, trying to decide how to proceed. She couldn't really show up with clothing for one and not the other. She had never seen Ben but imagined he had nothing better to wear than Laney.

She glanced down at the items still lying on the counter. One outfit each was better than what they had now. And she could come back next month and get another set.

Snatching up one shirt and one pair of blue jeans, she walked back to the shelf containing the clothing items and selected a larger pair of jeans. Turning to Mr. Tucker, she held them up for his perusal. "Do you think these are about the right size for Ben?"

Squinting, he studied the jeans, then nodded. "Yep. I'd say so."

"All right." Tarah selected a shirt she thought might be the same size Luke wore and strode with purpose back to the counter. "One outfit each will have to do, I suppose."

"You buying trousers for the little girl, too?"

"Yes, sir. I doubt I could get her to wear a dress."

"Suppose you're right about that."

"About the washtub, Mr. Tucker . . ."

He smacked his hand down on the counter and scowled. "Now hold on just a minute."

Tarah drew a breath and steeled herself for the scolding she knew was forthcoming.

"One set of duds ain't enough for a couple of growing young'uns. Get on back over there and pick out another set for each of 'em."

If he'd asked her to marry him, Tarah couldn't have been more shocked, especially after her discussion with Anthony about Mr. Tucker's attitude toward the children's pa.

"But . . ." Her face flushed hotly.

"Go on and do as I say."

"I'm sorry, Mr. Tucker, but I only have enough money to pay for these and maybe the washtub, if it isn't too much. You never gave me the price."

His scowl deepened. He marched over to the wall and grabbed the washtub, then stopped, snatching up two more sets of clothing, and flung the whole lot onto the counter. Next he moved to the rack of coats Tarah had been eyeing, chose two, and set those on the counter, as well. "Now anything else you can think of they might be needin' to get through the winter?"

"I — I really don't know." She also didn't know how she would pay for the items piled up on the countertop. "D–do you think I could open an account?"

"What for? Your pa already has one."

"No. I mean for me. In my name."

"I'd have to talk it over with your pa first," he said. "He might not like the idea of your buying things on credit."

"Then, Mr. Tucker, I'm afraid you'll have to put back the coats and one set of clothing for each child."

With a grunt, he began to fill a wooden

crate with the items, completely ignoring her protests.

Desperately Tarah offered him the few bills in her hand — every cent she had to her name. "Please, I'm trying to tell you I don't have enough money for all of those things."

He stopped what he was doing and wagged a bony finger toward her nose. "Now look here, missy. I'm not takin' one red cent from you. And that's my final word on the matter."

"I don't understand."

"It's no secret I don't have much use for a man who won't take care of his own. That Jenkins comes around here wanting credit for tobaccy and elixir when he can't get liquor anywhere else, and he tries to get other useless things that won't help those young'uns of his one bit. Oh, he'll throw in a pound of beans or an egg or two, just to make it look like he's trying to do for his family, but I know better. And I'm not givin' him any more credit in my store. But these shirts and such are for them youngsters, and that's different." Apparently finished having his say, he resumed the task of packing the crate.

Tears pooled in Tarah's eyes. "Thank you, Mr. Tucker. The children will be grateful."

His gaze darted back to hers. "Now don't be tellin' anyone I wouldn't take your money. Folks might come around lookin' for a handout."

A smile tugged the corners of Tarah's mouth. "My lips are sealed. I promise."

"Good. I'll hold ya to that. Now let me carry these out to your wagon for ya."

Clapping a hand to her cheek, Tarah let out a groan. "I walked to school this morning."

"You mean you're aimin' to carry this stuff all the way to the Jenkins place?"

"I — I didn't really think about it."

With a shake of his head, he reached under the counter and produced a key. "Come with me." A deep frown etched his brow, and his voice was close to a growl. "You can use my wagon, but bring it back tomorra." He walked to the door, muttering to himself. "Gonna have to lock up the store and most likely lose customers while I hitch up the team. Women . . ."

With great interest and more than a little curiosity, Anthony watched Tarah and Mr. Tucker cross the road and head toward the livery. The unlikely pair stood out like a snowy day in July. Mr. Tucker carried a crate in the crook of one thin arm and a bulky washtub in the other. Matching his stride, Tarah spoke with animated gestures, her face bright and smiling. Wishing he could hear their words, Anthony's curiosity suddenly got the better of him.

"Amos," he called to the smithy, "I'll be back in a minute."

The smithy nodded and resumed his pounding on a new pair of shoes for Anthony's saddle horse.

With purpose, Anthony strode the few yards to the livery and stepped inside. He found Tarah speaking pleasantly to Mr. Collins while Tucker hitched up his team.

"Howdy, Preacher." Mr. Collins glanced over Tarah's shoulder and grinned. "How's it goin'?"

"Just fine."

A touch of pink tinged Tarah's cheeks as she smiled a greeting. "What are you doing in town this time of day?"

"My horse threw a shoe." He jerked a thumb toward the smithy. "Amos is getting him all fixed up."

"All set." Mr. Tucker grabbed the bridle of one of the horses and led his team toward the door.

Tarah, Mr. Collins, and Anthony followed until they stood outside the livery.

"Thank you," Tarah said, beaming at the

storekeeper. "I promise you'll have your wagon back first thing in the morning. And thank you so much for —"

Raising a weathered hand, Tucker gave her a stern frown. "Now we had a deal. Don't go blabbing."

Lips twitching, Tarah nodded. "I almost spilled the beans, didn't I? I'll have to be more careful."

Anthony's jaw dropped as she raised on tiptoes and brushed her lips to Tucker's wrinkled face. Surprise lit the older man's eyes, then a scowl deepened the lines on his face. "I don't know where you got your manners, going around kissin' people without bein' invited."

A beguiling flush raced to Tarah's cheeks. Anthony's eyes flitted to her full mouth, and he suddenly wished that the kiss had been for him.

Mr. Collins chortled. "Probably the first time you ever been kissed in your life, Tucker. Probably be the last time, too." He gave Tarah a teasing wink. "If I'da known the pretty teacher was passing out kisses, I'da offered to let her use my wagon."

With an indignant snort, Mr. Tucker scowled. "There ain't no need to embarrass the girl, Collins. Move on outta my way so's I can help her into the wagon and get back to my store 'fore I lose any more custom-ers."

"Sure you don't want me to help her?" Collins baited the old codger. "She might try to kiss you again."

Anthony's chuckle earned him a reprov-ing frown from Tarah, whose face now glowed red. Averting his gaze, he cleared his throat and tried to stop grinning, to no avail. He looked back at Tarah and shrugged an apology. The sight of Mr. Tucker's outraged face was too much. Any moment, Anthony thought, the older man might call Collins out.

Tarah finally found her voice. Her eyes sparked fire. "Gentlemen, I assure you I won't be kissing Mr. Tucker again today. Furthermore, I am perfectly capable of get-ting myself into a wagon." So saying, she hoisted herself up onto the seat and grabbed the reins. "If you'll excuse me, I'll be on my way."

With a stubborn toss of her head, she flapped the reins and maneuvered the horses onto the cut-out road through town.

"Now see what you went and did," Mr. Tucker shot at the liveryman. "She's madder'n a hornet."

Anthony stepped forward before another argument ensued. He clapped a hand on

Tucker's shoulder. "I'll walk you across the street. I think I see someone trying to get into the store. You'd hate to lose a paying customer."

"True." He gave Mr. Collins one last look and pointed a bony finger. "Now don't you go blabbin' about that kiss. No need to have folks talkin'." Without waiting for an answer, he spun around and headed back to the mercantile.

Anthony followed. "See you later, Mr. Collins," he called over his shoulder. As soon as they were out of earshot, he turned to Tucker.

"Mr. Tucker, I've been meaning to ask you a favor."

The elderly man glanced up, suspicion clouding his face. "What kind of favor, Preacher?"

Anthony cleared his throat. "I was just thinking you might need some help around the store. With new people coming into town, I've noticed you're getting busier all the time."

Mr. Tucker nodded. "That's a fact. You lookin' for another job? I heard preachin's not goin' too good for you."

Heat crept up Anthony's neck. "The job wouldn't be for me."

"Who, then?"

144

"There's a young man, a schoolboy actually, who lost his father last year. The family is in dire straits, so I was thinking maybe you could hire him to work here afternoons and Saturdays."

"That's a fine idea, Preacher. Fact is, I been thinkin' of hirin' someone to clean up the place and help stock supplies. What's this young feller's name?"

Anthony averted his gaze. "Jeremiah."

"That Daniels boy?" Mr. Tucker regarded Anthony as though he'd suddenly lost his mind. "You know as well as I do he'd rob me blind. That kid steals from me every time he steps through the door. If his ma wasn't such a good woman, I'd have turned him over to the sheriff a long time ago."

"I know, Mr. Tucker, but maybe the boy just needs a man to look up to. A father figure of sorts."

Mr. Tucker let out a loud snort. "I ain't never been no father, and I don't need to start now."

"I know, but you are a good man. Just the sort of man a boy like Jeremiah can learn from."

The storekeeper seemed to consider it for a moment. "I'll think on it, but I ain't makin' no promises."

"I appreciate it," Anthony said.

145

Mr. Tucker opened the door. "No tellin' how many customers I lost while I hitched up the team for that girl," he grumbled.

"What's Tarah doing with your wagon, anyway?"

"Guess that's her business." Tucker gave him a sideways glance. " 'Course, it might not be a good idea for her to go out to the Jenkinses' place all by herself. That fella's a no-account if I ever met one."

"Tarah's going out to the Jenkinses' alone?"

"Well, I couldn't close my store and drive her out there, now, could I? I got customers countin' on me."

A lump lodged in Anthony's throat as images of a drunken Jenkins mauling Tarah invaded his mind.

"I'm going after her."

"Might not be a bad idea, at that."

Anthony said a hurried good-bye and broke into a jog as he made his way back to the smithy, praying his horse was ready to go. Thankfully he found Dodger tied up and waiting for him when he got there. Mounting quickly, he glanced down at the smithy. "Put it on my account, Amos. I'm in a hurry."

"Sure thing, Anthony."

Anthony nudged the horse into a trot and

headed toward the Jenkinses' place. He nearly groaned when Louisa's high-pitched voice hailed him from the porch of her parents' home at the edge of town. "Yoo-hoo, Anthony."

Knowing he couldn't pretend not to see her, Anthony heaved a sigh. He reined in Dodger, determined not to allow Louisa to keep him talking so long that Tarah would reach the soddy before he could catch up to her.

"Where are you off to in such a hurry?" Louisa called from the porch.

"Got some business out at the Jenkinses' place."

Wrinkling her nose, Louisa shuddered. "That awful place! Anthony, what possible business could you have out there?"

"Personal business." He smiled to take the sting from his words.

Sparks shot from her eyes, and she jerked her chin. "I don't think that place is very sanitary. And that awful child! She deserves a good spanking, if you ask me."

Which he most certainly hadn't. "I think learning about Jesus would do Laney a sight more good than a spanking."

As if sensing his irritation, Louisa smiled invitingly. "We don't have to talk about her, do we? Why don't you come down from there and join me in a nice cup of tea?" she said. "Rosa made some delicious molasses cookies earlier."

"I'm sorry, Louisa," he replied, knowing she could hear the distraction in his voice. He glanced toward the direction Tarah had taken. "I really have to go. Maybe another time."

"Oh, come now, just one little solitary cup of tea? I'll be so hurt if you refuse me."

Hesitating for only a moment at her pleading tone, Anthony shook his head. "I can't today. I'm sorry."

He held his breath as her face clouded over. All he needed was for Louisa to throw a temper tantrum in public. But her angry frown cleared so quickly, Anthony wondered if he'd imagined it.

Fingering the lace on her high-collared neckline, she gave him a pretty smile. "All right. I suppose I can wait until our picnic on Sunday to have you all to myself."

Anthony groaned inwardly. He'd forgotten about the picnic he'd promised her. Knowing he couldn't back out now, he simply nodded and tipped his hat.

"I'll be seeing you, then."

"Bye now."

With a relieved sigh, Anthony left her behind and urged Dodger into a full gallop.

CHAPTER 8

"Tarah, stop!"

The near panic in Anthony's voice sent Tarah's heart racing. She halted the team and spun around in her seat to wait for him to catch up. "What on earth is the matter?"

"Are you crazy?" he thundered, a deep frown creasing his brow.

"I don't know what you mean."

"What were you thinking, driving out to the Jenkinses' by yourself?"

Taken aback by his accusatory tone, Tarah's temper flared. "I have things to deliver for the children. Besides, why shouldn't I go out there alone?"

He slapped his hand against his thigh with a resounding *smack*. "The man's a drunk and a ne'er-do-well, Tarah. You don't know what he might be capable of doing."

"Honestly." Tarah dismissed his words with a wave of her hand, though she had to admit his concern thrilled her to the core.

"You heard Laney say her pa sleeps the day away. He probably won't wake up for a couple of hours yet."

"You don't know that for sure."

"I do know if we sit here arguing all day, there's a pretty good chance I'll catch him awake."

"Let's go, then. If he wakes up, I can speak to him about our idea to help with repairs to the homestead."

She cut her gaze upward and flashed a coquettish smile. "Why, Anthony, did you come all the way out here just to accompany me?" she asked in a singsong voice that would have put Louisa Thomas to shame.

His lips twitched, and one eyebrow shot upward. "I wasn't exactly planning to sling you over my shoulder and force you back to town."

Stung by his less-than-flattering response to her attempt at flirting, Tarah tossed her head. "I'd like to see you try," she challenged. "Besides, you needn't have bothered. I'm perfectly capable of taking care of myself."

"I'm sure you're right," he drawled. "But just in case, I think I'll tag along."

"Suit yourself." She flapped the reins to nudge the horses forward.

Astride Dodger, Anthony stayed beside

the wagon. Silence hung between them like a heavy fog.

Tarah felt like a fool for believing that just because Anthony worried about her safety, he was growing to care for her as a man cares for a woman. Louisa had set her cap for him, and obviously he had put up no resistance.

Still, in her mind, Tarah replayed the image she often conjured up these days — of Anthony realizing Louisa was not the woman for him. Of his declaring what a fool he'd been and begging Tarah to forgive him and be his wife.

Anthony's voice broke through. "What's in the box?"

Pulled from her dreams of a white gown made of silk and lace, Tarah jumped at the intrusion. "Pardon me?"

"The box? What are you delivering to Laney and Ben?"

"Oh. Some clothes I picked up at Tucker's."

"I thought we were going to ask for donations."

The memory of Laney's humiliation came rushing back, and Tarah spoke with conviction. "We were. But I didn't want Laney to wear the other children's cast-off clothing. I seriously doubt she would anyway."

"Sounds like you are encouraging her to be prideful," Anthony admonished.

Tarah frowned. "I don't mean to, Anthony. But Laney showed up at school today, and the children were horrible to her."

"Not Jo," he said with a groan.

She nodded. "Among others."

"I'm going to have to wear the tar out of that girl. She promised no more shenanigans."

"In this case, it wasn't only Jo. Laney is rather . . . offensive in some ways."

"So I've noticed," he said wryly.

Tarah rose to the girl's defense. "It isn't her fault. She's been raised without a mother to teach her how to bathe and dress. We can't expect her to come by such things naturally with the pa she's got."

"You're right, of course." He grinned. "I hope you got plenty of lye soap to go along with that washtub."

A gasp escaped her lips. "Honestly, Anthony, I forgot all about soap."

Anthony chuckled. "Plain water's not going to do much to cut through all that dirt."

Though tempted to turn the wagon toward home and beg soap from Ma, Tarah put the thought from her mind. Doing so would take another half hour at least, and she didn't want to take a chance on Mr.

Jenkins waking before she returned.

"Well, there's nothing to be done about that now. Maybe we can get the first couple of layers off, anyway."

The sound of Anthony's laughter filled the air with a pleasant ring. "Tarah, you're some fine woman. That girl is blessed to have found you."

Her heart soared at the compliment. "I can't help but believe God brought Laney into my life. I was feeling like such a failure as a teacher and just about ready to give up," she confided. "Then, from nowhere, Laney appeared at the river, so obviously in need of love and care. I just knew she was a child I could help."

"God has a way of lifting us from our own problems by showing us how much greater need exists in the world."

The homestead loomed before them, the squalor once again causing Tarah to cringe. Laney stood outside, along with an equally dirty boy who could only be Ben.

"Howdy, Tarah." Laney waved her hand wildly.

Tarah waved back and smiled. "Hello!" She slowed the horses to a stop and wrapped the reins around the brake. Anthony dismounted Dodger and hurried to the wagon.

She accepted his proffered hand, thrilling

at the warmth of his touch as their fingers met. Pulled into the depth of his gaze, Tarah climbed down, unable to breathe.

Rather than dropping her hand immediately as propriety demanded, Anthony tightened his grip, causing her pulse to quicken. Oh, how she wished he would draw her into the strength of his arms! As if reading her thoughts, he took a step closer.

Laney's voice brought Tarah to her senses. "You make yer girl stay home this time, Preacher?"

Tarah snatched her hand away and quickly averted her gaze. *Idiot!* she chided herself. *It's Louisa, not you, Anthony wants.*

"I told you, she's not my girl," Anthony insisted.

Laney smirked. "She'll get her claws in you — 'lessen you get smart and send her packin'."

Tarah couldn't disagree with Laney's assessment, but from Anthony's pleading gaze, she knew he expected her to bail him out of the embarrassing predicament. "Laney," she said firmly, "that's Reverend Greene's business. Why don't you introduce me to the handsome young man with you?"

An impish grin split Laney's face. "Don't see no han'some young man 'round here." She elbowed the suddenly red-faced boy.

"Ain't nobody but my brother, Ben, near as I can tell."

"Aw, hush up, Laney," Ben said, keeping his eyes on his dirty bare feet.

Boots! Tarah groaned inwardly. These children were both barefoot. Why hadn't she thought of buying boots while Mr. Tucker was being so generous?

Stepping forward, she extended her hand. "It's a pleasure to meet you, Ben. I'm Miss St. John. The schoolteacher."

Tarah hadn't planned to bring up the subject of Ben attending school until she had convinced Laney to come back. But the eager light in his eyes spurred her to do just that. "I'd love to see you in school. I have a brother I'll bet is just about your age. Are you twelve?"

"Fourteen."

So he, too, was small for his age.

"Luke will be thirteen soon. That's pretty close to your age. So you see? You already have something in common."

A loud snort from Laney drew Tarah's attention from Ben. "I ain't goin' back to that school, Tarah. And neither is Ben."

"You don't tell me where I am or ain't goin', Laney," Ben said hotly. "Iffen I want to go to school, I'm goin'."

"Then yer about as dumb as Pa says. I

155

tol' ya what them kids said to me. All pluggin' up their noses and sayin' how I was dirty and all."

"They was right. Ya are dirty, and I don't blame 'em for pluggin' up their noses. Ya stink!"

"I ain't takin' none of yer insults." Laney flew at Ben, the force of her weight knocking him off his already unstable feet. She landed atop him. Fists flying, she made little or no contact before his arms came around her, pinning her arms to her sides. "If you don't settle down, I'm gonna have to tie you up."

Tarah looked helplessly at Anthony. He gaped at the pair, disbelief plastered across his face.

"Honestly, Anthony. Do something."

"Sorry," he muttered. "I just can't believe . . ." He shook his head and stepped forward. Grabbing Laney around the waist, he pulled her off Ben.

"Let go of me!" she hollered, twisting and kicking.

Anthony set her on the ground, keeping a firm hold on her arms. "Simmer down."

Raring back, Laney gave him a sound kick in the shin.

"Ow!" Anthony growled. "Why, you little —"

"No one tells me what to do. 'Specially not no preacher."

"Good grief." Tarah shook her head at the spectacle. How in the world had the situation gotten so out of hand? "Laney, would you like to know why I'm here?"

Sudden interest flickered in her eyes, then her face clouded over. "I figure yer here to try and get my pa to make me go to school. But it won't do no good," she said, setting her jaw stubbornly. "I don't go where I ain't wanted. 'Sides, ain't seen Pa 'round here since yesterday. We figure he probably got locked up again."

Tarah caught Anthony's gaze, noting his look of bewilderment, which in all likelihood matched her own.

"You've been all alone since yesterday?" she asked incredulously, thinking of her own small brothers and sisters. "What have you eaten?"

"Aw, Tarah," Laney said, kicking at the ground. "Don't go worryin' about us. Me and Ben can take care of ourselves."

"Now that sounds familiar," Anthony said, the corners of his lips curving into a wry grin.

Tarah felt herself blush. "I'm not exactly a child." She turned her attention back to Laney and Ben. "I'm sure you're very self-reliant —"

"We ain't neither!"

"Hush up, Laney," Ben commanded. "The teacher means we can take care of ourselves."

"Well, ain't that what I just said?"

"Honestly." How would she ever get these children to accept help? Their fierce pride radiated through dirty faces and showed strongly in the stance of their thin bodies.

Helpless fury swept through her, and she had a strong urge to snatch up the pair and take them home with her — kicking and screaming if need be.

Anthony's grip on her elbow brought her to her senses, and she drew a long, slow breath to steady her raging emotions.

"You can't stay alone out here with no food." She waited for the outrage, but mercifully, it didn't come. The children stared at her curiously, as though awaiting the alternative. "So I wondered if you would mind coming home with me — just until your pa comes back."

"Pa'll whale the daylights out of us iffen we ain't here when he gets back," Laney piped up.

"We'll convince your pa that we insisted."

Hope shone in both pairs of eyes. Then Ben's face slowly clouded over with disappointment. "We cain't go, Teacher."

"Why not?"

"Yer folks ain't gonna want us sleepin' on their clean beds and eatin' at their table."

Laney cut her gaze to her brother. "Maybe we could sleep in the barn like we did that time Missus Avery tried to help out."

Crossing her arms across her chest, Tarah looked firmly from one child to the other. "You're not sleeping in the barn, and you're not staying here."

"There is the matter of cleanliness, Tarah." Anthony motioned toward the wagon with his head. "Might be awkward for them bathing at your house with all your brothers and sisters there."

Tarah smiled up at him, warmed by his sensitivity to the children's feelings. Of course the children needed to bathe first. There was no need to give Luke any more ammunition — just in case his good behavior today was a one-time reprieve.

"Hey, who says we're gonna take baths anyways? 'Sides, I done told you, Tarah, Pa kicked a hole in the washtub."

Reaching into the back of the wagon, Anthony produced the new washtub. "Here you go." His eyes twinkled at the expressions of dread on the two faces. "And there are new clothes for each of you where that came from."

Laney's mouth dropped open. "We got new clothes?"

"Yes," Tarah said with a smile. "Now you can come to school without worrying about the other kids making fun of you."

Suddenly Laney's face grew stormy. "Me and Ben don't need yer charity," she spat. "What we got on is just fine. Ya can take them clothes back to the folks they came from and tell 'em we said we don't want 'em."

Oh, Lord, thank You for instructing me to buy new clothing for these children.

"I can't take them back, Laney. They came from Tucker's."

"You got us new clothes?" Ben asked, a hesitant smile peeking around the edges of his mouth. "Really new?"

Tarah nodded. "I guessed at your sizes, so I hope they fit."

"Why'd ya go and do that, Tarah?" Laney asked.

"Because I don't want children to make fun of you. Because I want to see you come to school and learn." Tears sprang to her eyes. "Because I want you to have a chance to grow up and have a better life."

"Pity!" Laney spat.

"Love, Laney, honey," Anthony said softly.

160

"Not pity."

Tarah's breath caught in her throat at the sound of his voice. He, too, seemed choked up, and Tarah thought she might die of love for him right then and there. If the children weren't right under their noses, she would have thrown herself into his arms and begged him to love her back.

She turned back to Laney. All the thunder was gone from the child's face. "Well . . ."

"It's okay, Laney," Ben said, placing a gentle hand upon his little sister's arm. "Let's just take it. This ain't like other folks. I can tell the teacher ain't tryin' to make us feel bad. She just wants to help."

"We don't need her help," Laney mumbled, eyeing the crate Anthony held in his arms.

Ben gazed sadly into her eyes. "Yes, we do. Them britches yer wearin' are gonna come apart 'fore long, and then you'll be nekkid. And this shirt I'm wearin' only gots two buttons."

Folding her scrawny arms across her chest, Laney set her jaw stubbornly. "I don't want 'em if I gotta take a bath."

Tarah's lips twitched. The girl was softening. She looked to Ben, hoping he would keep talking sense into Laney.

A worried frown creased his brow. "Do

we *gotta* take a bath to get the new clothes?"

Swallowing hard, Tarah shook her head. "The new things belong to you, Ben. I won't dictate what you have to do in order to have them."

"Good." Laney gave a curt nod. "Reckon that settles things, then."

Tarah's heart sank to her toes.

"Wait, Laney." Ben's hesitant voice made Tarah's dashed hopes rise. "We gotta take a bath."

"What fer? Didn't you hear what Tarah just said? You was right. She ain't like them other folks."

The children continued their discourse as though Anthony and Tarah weren't present. Capturing her bottom lip between her teeth, Tarah caught Anthony's gaze. He winked and gave her a reassuring smile.

"Ain't nobody makin' me take a bath iffen I don't want one," Laney declared hotly, her fiery temper once more blazing.

"It ain't right to smell up them new clothes. 'Sides, we cain't go to Tarah's house like this." Ben glanced at Tarah, then back to Laney. "I know she's nicer than most folks, but that don't mean her ma and pa want us sleepin' in their clean beds."

"Aw, I'd rather sleep in the barn."

Ben grinned and nudged her with his

elbow. "Come on. Betcha can't get all that dirt off anyhow."

"Bet I can!"

"It's settled then." Anthony spoke up before another argument ensued. "Ben, come take this crate off my hands. Laney, can you warm water for the baths?"

"Guess I can do that, Preacher."

Ben limped forward and took the crate of clothes, his eyes growing wide at the sight of the wool coats. "Never had a coat that I recollect," he said in awe.

"We got coats in there, too? Lemme see." Suddenly Laney turned to Tarah, her nose scrunching in disgust. "Ya ain't aimin' to try and get me to wear no dress, are ya? 'Cause I ain't wearin' no dress, and ain't no one makin' me do —"

Tarah laughed outright. "Laney Jenkins, do you think I'd try to get you to wear anything you don't want to? There are two fine, sturdy pairs of blue jeans and two warm shirts just your size, I think."

Laney beamed. "Yep, ya sure ain't like them other folks." She followed after Ben, trying to grab at the new things.

"Keep yer dirty hands off my new coat!" Ben hollered.

"Sor—ry. Don't you be puttin' yer hands on my new coat neither, then."

"Anthony," Tarah said, once the children were out of earshot, "can you ride to my house and let Ma and Pa know I'll be along later with guests?"

Anthony scowled. "What if Jenkins comes around while I'm gone?"

"He won't. Besides, I need that soap — and I noticed them both scratching their heads. Better bring some kerosene just in case they have lice."

Anthony grimaced. "You're right."

"Oh, and ask Ma to send along some bread, too. These children probably haven't eaten all day. I want to get something into their stomachs to hold them over until we get them home."

Tenderness flickered in Anthony's eyes. He reached forward and brushed his fingertips along her cheek, sending a shiver up her spine. "I admire what you're doing for these children," he said. "You've become quite a woman, Tarah St. John."

Before she could respond, he mounted Dodger and took off toward the St. John ranch.

The moon hovered full and bright, and a smattering of stars dotted the sky by the time a weary and waterlogged Tarah climbed into the wagon with two very clean, bug-free children.

Laney had sputtered and protested, but Tarah insisted on helping the girl with her bath. They were forced to change the filthy water three times before no more dirt surfaced on her skin.

The child had let out a howl loud enough to put any warring Indian to shame while Tarah poured kerosene through her hair, then soaped the long tresses three times to remove the grime. Once clean, Tarah noticed Laney's hair wasn't brown or dark auburn as she had originally suspected. Laney had beautiful dark blond hair, with just a hint of curl at the ends.

The combing process was long and painful for the girl, who begged Tarah to simply chop it off like Ben's and be done with it. Tarah refused, and once the ordeal ended, she managed to convince Laney that two braids hanging on either side of her head would help keep her hair from matting up again.

Anthony repeated the process with Ben, although he gave the boy more privacy. But he took care of his hair and inspected the dirt removal process just to be certain the lad cleaned himself thoroughly.

The children fidgeted with pent-up anxiety on the ride to the ranch.

"I sure hope yer folks don't mind about

you invitin' us to yer house, Tarah," said Laney from the back of the wagon.

"They seem to be looking forward to it," Anthony answered for Tarah.

"Well, they ain't met us yet, Preacher," she shot back.

Tarah turned in the seat and gave the girl a reassuring smile. "I know they'll love you. Don't worry."

"Ain't worried. Just don't stay where I ain't wanted, that's all."

Tarah noticed Anthony's lips twitching and was hard-pressed to bite back her own laugh. Laney was the most stubborn child she had ever met. "I assure you, you are wanted at our home."

Laney let out a snort. "We'll see."

Both children were sound asleep by the time they made it to the ranch. Pa greeted them from his seat on the porch. "I was about to head over to the soddy and make sure everything was all right," he said.

"It took awhile to finish with baths," Tarah replied, glad to be home.

Anthony offered Pa his hand. "You needn't have worried. I wouldn't have let anything happen to her, sir."

Pa grinned. "No, I don't suppose you would. You two had better get those youngsters inside. I'll tie up Anthony's horse and take care of the team."

"Thank you, Pa."

Tarah gently woke Ben while Anthony gathered up Laney and carried her into the house.

Cassidy's face gentled at the sight of the tiny girl snoring lightly in Anthony's arms and Ben limping behind them, a wide, sleepy yawn stretching his thin mouth. She turned to the boy and took his hand. "I'm Tarah's ma, but you can call me Cassidy, unless you're more comfortable with Mrs. St. John. I'm delighted to have you with us."

"Thanks, ma'am. Me an' Laney 'preciate yer kindness."

"Think nothing of it. It's our pleasure. Are you hungry?"

"A mite."

"I have a pot of buffalo stew warming on the stove. You sit at the table there, and I'll be back in a jiffy." She turned to Tarah. "Show Anthony to Emily's bedroom. The covers are already turned down. I put Em in with you in Granny's room for the night."

In the bedroom, Anthony gently deposited Laney onto the bed. Tarah glanced down at the beautiful face bathed in moonlight shining in through the window. "She's lovely, isn't she?"

"Who would have ever thought beneath

all that dirt was such a pretty little girl?" Anthony said with a chuckle.

Tarah pulled up the quilt and tucked it securely around Laney's shoulders. The little girl moaned and shifted in her sleep. Anthony and Tarah remained motionless until she lay still and her steady breathing resumed.

Edging toward the door, Tarah motioned for Anthony to follow.

"Got her all settled in?" Cassidy asked when they reached the front room.

Tarah smiled and nodded. "She's sound asleep."

"Good. This fellow will be ready for bed as soon as he's eaten his fill."

Ben beamed at Cassidy. "This is mighty good cookin', ma'am." He reached up as if to swipe his sleeve across his mouth, then stopped, his gaze darting to Tarah. She smiled and inclined her head toward the napkin next to his plate.

"Will you stay and have some supper, Anthony?" Cassidy asked.

"I'd best be getting on home. Ma doesn't know where I am, and I'm sure she'll be worried."

Tarah swallowed her disappointment at his refusal. "I'll walk you out."

"Don't stay out too long, Tarah," Cassidy

said. "There's a chill in the air. We don't want you catching cold."

Warmth flooded Tarah's cheeks. Honestly. She didn't need to be treated like a baby right in front of Anthony. But she smiled and nodded, then slipped out the door ahead of him.

"I want to thank you for coming after me today," she said as they stepped into the star-filled night. "I couldn't have managed those children alone."

"My pleasure." Anthony's mouth curved into a smile. "You did a fine job. Although I think I've mentioned that a couple of times today."

"I think so. But I couldn't have done it without you."

Reaching out, he fingered a strand of hair, long since pulled loose from her chignon. "I guess we make a pretty good team."

"Yes," Tarah murmured, lifting her chin a little just in case he wanted to kiss her. "I suppose we do."

Anthony touched her shoulder, then her arm, until finally he took her hand in his. Warmth enveloped her, and a soft, unbidden sigh escaped her lips as Anthony pulled her ever so slightly forward.

A loud cough from the other side of the porch startled them, making Tarah jump.

Anthony dropped her hand and took a large step back.

"Guess you two didn't see me sitting here," Pa said with a chuckle.

Tarah's cheeks warmed, and she was glad for the cover of darkness to hide her humiliation.

"No, sir." Anthony's voice cracked like a twelve-year-old boy's.

"Didn't think so. I guess you'll be going now?"

"Yes, sir." Anthony turned to Tarah. "Good night. I'll see you in church on Sunday."

"We're looking forward to it," Pa said, a teasing lilt to his voice.

"Well, good night, then," he said, backing down the steps.

"Night, Anthony," Pa called, a little louder than he needed to, in Tarah's opinion.

A lump of disappointment lodged in her throat as Anthony mounted and rode away. Furious, she turned her gaze to Pa.

"Well, now," he said. "I couldn't have him kissing my little girl right in front of me, could I?"

"Oh, Pa."

"Now there'll be plenty of time for that if he ever says his piece and asks for your hand. And not before. Is that clear?"

"Yes, Pa." Tarah said a curt good night and stomped inside. She'd been sure she was about to get herself kissed. If only Pa hadn't been on the porch, she could have made Anthony forget all about Louisa Thomas!

CHAPTER 9

"Looks like we're not the only ones who thought a fall picnic was a good idea."

Tarah glanced up at the sound of Pa's voice. Dread engulfed her as she recognized the pair seated on a blanket a few yards from the river. She inwardly groaned at the sight.

"Unless my eyes are playing tricks on me," Pa said, thick amusement coloring his words, "I'd say that's Anthony and Louisa up ahead."

"And Josie," Luke piped in, excitement edging his voice. "Hi, Jo!"

From her spot at the riverbank, Josie grinned and waved. Luke hopped from the still-rolling wagon and sprinted to join her, leaving Cassidy to call after him to stay close by.

Tarah felt a low ember of indignation quickly give rise to an inferno of temper as Anthony's beseeching gaze reached out to her. With a jerk of her chin, she averted her gaze, letting him know just what she thought of the situation.

Nearly choked with tears, Tarah felt his betrayal to her toes. After all they had been through just two days ago, she had caught the two-timer having a chummy picnic with Louisa Thomas. And he called himself a preacher!

Seated next to his girl, Camilla, on the wagon flap, Sam gave Tarah an understanding smile. His compassionate gaze searched her face, sending a rush of heat to her cheeks. What did Sam know about unrequited love? He and Camilla had been in love since they were both fifteen years old. And now, seated together with a twin on each lap, they made a picture of domesticity.

Cringing, Tarah realized that Pa's comment a few weeks ago about Sam getting married first might actually come true. She gave Sam what she hoped to be a reassuring smile, then looked away to hide her humiliation.

Anthony rose from the blanket and stepped forward, waving in friendly greeting.

To Tarah's way of thinking, he looked just about as guilty as a dog caught with a

Christmas ham.

Obviously thinking the same thing, Pa gave a low chuckle.

"Dell . . . ," Cassidy lightly admonished.

Louisa rose and took her place next to Anthony. Her willowy hand slipped through his arm, and she challenged Tarah with a lift of one delicate eyebrow.

"What's *she* doin' here?" Laney asked, her perky nose wrinkling into a scowl. "That preacher's not too smart. I told him he oughtta send her packing."

Pa laughed outright.

"Dell!" Cassidy turned to the outspoken little girl. "Laney, honey, please don't be rude."

"But that lady ain't nothin' but a —" She broke off the flow of words, apparently thinking better of what she'd been about to say, and ducked her head in submission. "Yes, ma'am."

Resisting the urge to bolt, thus giving Louisa the pleasure of knowing she was upset, Tarah plastered a smile on her face and reined in Abby. She dismounted and tied the horse to the wagon.

"Looks like we're sharing a picnic spot," Pa said, extending a hand to Anthony. "That okay with you?"

"Of course." Anthony accepted the proffered hand and gave a short, dry cough.

"This is just wonderful," Louisa gushed, taking Hope from Sam's arms. Tarah scowled as the little girl went to Louisa without so much as a hint of protest. Her chubby hands grabbed on to a strawberry-blond ringlet. "Pwetty."

The little traitor!

Releasing an annoying giggle, Louisa planted a kiss on the little girl's cheek. "Look," she called to Anthony, who had joined Dell and Sam to help unload the food from the wagon. "She loves me."

"Aw, don't think yer nothin' special," Laney said, reaching up a hand to tickle Hope's belly. "She loves everybody. Don't ya, Hopey Wopey?" Hope laughed outright and threw her body toward Laney. "See?" With a smug grin, Laney took the toddler and headed toward the blanket Cassidy had spread on the ground.

With a great sense of satisfaction, Tarah watched Louisa's cheeks grow red. She silently blessed Laney for putting the bothersome woman in her place. But her guilt got the better of her, and she gave Louisa a genuine hint of a smile. "You three might as well eat with us," she offered, to take away the sting of Laney's rudeness.

"I don't suppose we have a choice," Louisa hissed, "although we'd much rather be alone. It was bad enough we had to bring Anthony's horror of a niece along with us."

A gasp escaped Tarah's lips, and she felt her eyes growing wide. "We certainly didn't interrupt your little outing just to inconvenience you. My family has been coming to this picnic spot twice a year for the last three years. And Anthony doesn't seem at all bothered by our presence."

Louisa's nostrils flared in anger. "Don't think I can't figure out what you're up to."

"I don't know what you mean."

Pursing her lips, Louisa narrowed her eyes. "Come now, don't act innocent with me. We're both women, and we both know what we want. Or rather whom we want. The difference is I already have him. And you never will." She spun on her heel and flounced away to join the others.

Tarah stared after her, fuming and wishing she could refute the other girl's words. Though it grated on her to admit it, Louisa had spoken truthfully. She had staked her claim on Anthony, and it appeared he had no desire to be rescued from her clutches. That was his misfortune, Tarah thought stubbornly. Louisa would make him miserable in the long run, and it served him right for being so ignorant of the ways of women.

"Teacher?"

"What?" she asked in a clipped voice, turning to find Ben standing next to her, looking as if he'd been slapped. "Oh, Ben, I'm sorry. It's not you."

"I heard them things she said to you."

Chafed from the knowledge that this child had witnessed her humiliation, Tarah planted her hands on her hips and frowned. "It's not nice to eavesdrop."

"I wasn't. Just heard it, that's all. Anyways," he murmured, "I wanted to tell ya not to believe what she said. It ain't true."

He started to limp away, but Tarah placed a restraining hand on his arm. "Wait. What do you mean?"

A shrug lifted his bony shoulders. "Preacher ain't gonna ask her to marry him. Near as I can tell, he don't care too much for her."

Tarah's heart soared, then plummeted. What did a fourteen-year-old boy know about love? "Thank you for trying to make me feel better, but you needn't worry. Reverend Greene is perfectly free to court whomever he pleases, and it's immaterial to me."

The look of disbelief covering his face brought a fresh rush of heat to Tarah's cheeks, but she stood her ground. "Anthony and I have known each other for several years," she insisted. "There's nothing but friendship between us."

The boy's gaze darted over her shoulder, and his eyes widened.

"Really, Ben. It's not very polite to look past someone when they're speaking to you."

"Sorry, Teacher."

"Oh, it's all right. I just hope you understand that whatever Louisa said to me doesn't matter, because I'm not interested in Anthony as a beau. You see? He's just a good friend."

Tarah released an impatient sigh as the boy's gaze drifted past her once again. "Honestly, Ben." She twisted to see what he found so interesting.

A knot formed in the pit of her stomach as she realized why Ben had been so antsy. With a sinking feeling, she wondered just how long Anthony had been standing less than five feet behind her.

Anthony tried to concentrate on his food but found his stomach recoiling at the sight of the meal Louisa had prepared. The talking and laughter from the merry group of picnickers buzzed around him unintelligibly, and he wished for a quick end to the day so he could salvage his wounded pride in private. How could he have been so mistaken about Tarah's feelings for him?

If Dell hadn't interrupted two nights ago, he would have taken Tarah into his arms, and he had the feeling — or had had at the time — that she would have allowed a small kiss before all was said and done. He glanced at her now, observing the fact that she struggled with her appetite just as he did.

As if sensing his eyes studying her, she lifted her head, a question written on her lovely face.

Dear Father in heaven, he prayed, the shock of revelation shooting down his spine, *I'm in love.*

Sorrow, combined with question, filled her eyes. Anthony wanted to look away but found that he couldn't escape the violet depths of her gaze. Surely she knew how he felt. He could shoulder her anger, swallow her disdain, or accept her love, but her pity he could not and would not abide.

Just as he was about to excuse himself from the company, he heard Josie speak up. "Ma says we're going back east as soon as the school term is up. Isn't that right, Uncle Anthony?"

Dragging his gaze from Tarah's, Anthony

nodded. "Ma's doing much better. Ella is anxious to get home before the baby arrives, but she wants to let the children finish out the term first."

"Tarah, I imagine you're relieved the school term will be over soon," Louisa piped in. "I hear things haven't gone well."

Tarah flushed and glared at Anthony. Indignation swelled his chest at the accusation in her eyes. Did she really think he had betrayed her confidence about his unruly niece and her brother?

Louisa pressed on before Tarah could answer. "Perhaps the town council will give someone else a chance to teach the children since you apparently aren't enjoying the position." She cast a hopeful sidelong glance at Dell.

"Tarah's the best teacher alive," Laney declared hotly.

"How would you know?" Josie's voice rang with challenge. "You didn't stay at school long enough to sit down, much less see her teach."

Laney's eyes narrowed dangerously, her lips pushing out from her face. "Tarah's a sight better'n *anybody* could be in a million years. And I ain't gotta go to no school to figure that out. And iffen anyone's callin' me a liar, I'll knock 'em flat."

"That won't be necessary, little lightning bolt." Dell cleared his throat and eyed Louisa with a stern glance. "I reckon the job for next term will be Tarah's if she wants to accept it. The council has heard no complaints about her teaching."

Color flooded Louisa's cheeks, and she ducked her head.

"Oh, honestly. I probably won't be here to teach another term anyway." Tarah shot to her feet. "I had planned to discuss this with Ma and Pa privately, but since you all feel so comfortable speaking about my life, I guess I'll just go ahead and tell you."

Dread filled Anthony at her words, and he waited impatiently while she paused to take a breath.

"Tell us what, Tarah?" Cassidy asked, her brow furrowing.

"I received a letter Friday from Mr. Halston —"

"Clyde Halston? From Starling?" Dell asked. "Why would he write to you?"

Anthony wanted to know the same thing. A surge of jealousy shot through him at the thought of another man courting Tarah.

"It seems Starling has come into some funds to build a small school and hire a teacher. And he suggested me."

"But that's nearly twenty miles away!"

Cassidy's frown deepened. "I don't think it's such a good idea."

"Darling," Dell said gently, placing a hand on her arm. "Our little girl is old enough to make this decision on her own."

"Now hold on!" Laney hopped to her feet and stood facing Tarah, her features twisted into a scowl. "Ya just cain't get a body to goin' to school and then up and leave 'em. I ain't goin' if *she's* teachin'." She tossed her head toward Louisa without moving her gaze from Tarah.

Tarah's face softened considerably as she stared down at the little ball of fire. "I will finish out my term in Harper." She glanced back up, her eyes shifting between Dell and Cassidy. "They're building the schoolhouse now and would want me to start teaching a winter term. Mr. Halston said the town has the funds to pay a teacher for five months." Tarah glanced around the circle of family and friends, and her voice faltered. "Th– they want me to come right after the new year."

"But, Tarah, you can't go." Emily's lips trembled, her wide green eyes regarding Tarah sorrowfully. "We'd miss you something awful if you left home."

"Oh, honey. I'd miss you, too. But —"

"Well, I think it would be a wonderful opportunity for Tarah," Louisa said brightly.

"Yer just sayin' that 'cuz you wanna steal her job out from under her." The look of disdain on Laney's face could have melted the strongest of men, but Louisa opened her mouth as though ready to take on the tiny creature.

"Laney," Cassidy said before Louisa could voice her retort, "you owe Miss Thomas an apology."

The child stamped her foot and glared at Louisa.

Anthony thought he detected a note of triumph in Louisa's returning gaze. Laney must have detected the same thing, for she jerked her chin and planted her hands firmly on her tiny hips. "Ain't no way I'm gonna 'pologize to her. I stand by what I said, and ain't nobody gonna make me say nothin' else!" With that, she dashed off toward the river, leaving the group around the blanket to stare in disbelief.

"I'll go after her," Tarah offered.

"Well, I certainly hope you give her a good talking to," Louisa said indignantly. "What a spoiled child!"

Anthony shook his head as his anger surged. "Laney is the least spoiled child I've ever known. It's ridiculous to even say such a thing." Louisa's mouth dropped as

Anthony continued. "And I don't believe I'd be remiss in pointing out that she has a wisdom about human nature that many of us lack."

He caught Tarah's wide-eyed gaze. "Would you mind if I go after Laney and have a talk with her?" he asked.

"I — I guess not."

"I'm goin', too." Ben stood beside Anthony. "She can get awfully stubborn."

With a nod, Anthony set off toward the river with Ben close on his heels. He found Laney seated on the bank, tossing stray twigs into the rippling water.

She dashed a tear from her cheek and didn't bother to glance up as Anthony dropped to the ground beside her. Ben took the space on her other side. "I stand by what I said, and I ain't 'pologizin' to that hoity-toit even if she is yer girl. So you can fergit it, Preacher. And you ain't talkin' me into it, Ben. I don't care if Tarah's folks kick us out, neither."

Anthony chuckled. "I didn't come here to try to get you to apologize. You don't need to worry about Tarah's folks kicking you out. And how many times do I have to tell you Louisa's not my girl?"

Laney snorted. "Then yer the only one who don't think so." She tossed a twig into the water. "I even heard that Josie say you'll most likely marry up with her."

"Well, my niece is wrong."

"I wouldn't bet on it if I was you."

Ben kept silent through the exchange. He met Anthony's gaze over Laney's head and held on as though trying to read into the depths of his soul. Anthony looked away from the wizened perusal and released a frustrated sigh. "I didn't come over here to discuss me, anyway."

"Then what'd you want to talk about?"

Suddenly Anthony didn't know. He wanted to reassure her. To gather her in his lap and give her the kind of love a child deserved. Reaching into his heart, he asked the first question that came to mind. "You two haven't been to church much, have you?"

"Ain't never been b'fore today."

"What did you think of the service?"

Laney shrugged. "Don't rightly know. My b'hind got sore sittin' there so long. Ya yelled real good, though. Just like Pa when he's all liquored up."

Anthony felt the heat creep up his neck. He turned toward Ben, suddenly caring what the child thought.

Ben frowned.

With a sinking heart, Anthony gave him a

wry smile. "You didn't care for the service either, I take it?"

"Reckon I did," he said quietly.

"You enjoyed the sermon?"

"Cain't rightly say I understood a lot of it. But the part about bein' sinners and how we need God — that part I understood. 'Course, I reckon Laney and me was the only ones in the whole church that didn't already know it."

"What do you mean?"

"You talkin' 'bout that fella that kept talkin' in front of us, Ben?"

Ben nodded.

Anthony waited for someone to elaborate and was just about to suggest it when Laney obliged. "Kept sayin' how there weren't no real sinners in the whole place and how you was spittin' in the wind."

Embarrassment swept over Anthony. Did the whole town believe he was preaching in vain? Didn't Paul say, "All have sinned and come short of the glory of God"? Or was it Peter? Anthony's muddled brain couldn't conjure up a single verse of scripture he could quote with certainty. He raked his fingers through his hair. "I just don't know what to do." Realizing he'd spoken aloud, his gaze darted to the two children. They stared back at him, curiosity on Laney's face, understanding on Ben's. The boy gave a hesitant frown and looked away.

"It's all right, Ben. You can speak your mind."

"Naw."

Curiosity piqued, Anthony felt compelled to hear what the boy had to say. "Go ahead," he urged. "I won't be angry."

Ben took a long breath, then released it with a *whoosh*. "Seems to me," he began earnestly, "that tryin' to tell folks who already go to church that they need God is sorta like tryin' to talk a hound dog into eatin' a rabbit. He already knows a rabbit's good eatin'."

Defenses raised, Anthony stared at Ben. What did this kid know about anything? The strongest lesson Reverend Cahill had taught Anthony was to hammer the salvation message into his congregation. "Many church folks think their lives are just fine," Anthony's mentor had said, "when in reality, they're closer to the gates of hell than they know. As ministers of the gospel, it's our responsibility not to let even the smallest opportunity pass without sharing the truth. And that will more than likely make you unpopular."

Well, it had certainly made Anthony unpopular. His three-month trial period was half over, and he worried he might not have his position extended to a permanent status — despite the fact that he'd visited each of the remaining families this week.

He took comfort from the memory of Reverend Cahill's words. "Always preach the truth, no matter the cost. It's better to lose man's favor than to stand before God and answer why you took the easy road."

With his arms behind him, he leaned on his palms and stared reflectively into the water.

"Sorry, Preacher. I shoulda kept my mouth shut."

"No, Ben," he said. "You pretty much summed up the reason my congregation has been getting smaller and smaller each week. But you have to understand. Not everyone attends church services for the right reasons. There are many people sitting on benches week after week who don't know the Lord."

"And you figure some of them are sittin' in yer church?"

Anthony shrugged. "I can't see the hearts of men. I only have to preach what I feel God is telling me to preach."

"So yer not mad?"

Anthony smiled. "Not a bit. I think you're a very bright boy with a lot of insight."

Ben flushed with pleasure.

"Anthony?" Louisa's soft voice behind him drew Anthony's attention from his new-found revelation.

"I'm leavin'." Laney shot to her feet and stomped away.

"The boys are planning to play baseball, if you'd like to join them," Louisa offered to Ben as he stood.

"I cain't." He limped away, leaving a red-faced Louisa to stare after him.

"I hoped perhaps we could take a walk while the children are playing," she said, her voice more subdued than Anthony had ever observed.

"Let's sit here for a while instead."

She eyed the ground dubiously, then nodded. "If that's what you prefer." Carefully she lowered herself until she sat beside him. "I know you didn't mean to speak to me the way you did earlier," she said, a hint of her usual cheerfulness returning. "So I've decided to forgive you."

"That's good of you," Anthony drawled. He had intended to apologize for admonishing her in front of the St. Johns, but apparently an apology wasn't necessary.

"Hey, Anthony!"

Anthony turned at the sound of Luke's voice.

"Come play baseball with us. We need a

pitcher."

"Oh, Anthony." Louisa's countenance took on a pretty pout. "You're not going to play with the children, are you?"

Relieved at the chance to make a graceful exit, Anthony stood and grinned down at her. "You heard Luke. They need a pitcher."

He heard her huff as he strode toward the players. A niggling of unease swept over him at the thought of the entire town believing they were courting. He wasn't sure how to go about it, but he had to find a way to let Louisa know she had to look elsewhere for a husband. Of course, if she had her heart set on marrying him, as Laney seemed to think she did, he would probably have an easier time trying to convince a rattlesnake not to strike.

Releasing a heavy sigh, Anthony tried to push away his troublesome thoughts. Between Louisa's relentless pursuit, his congregation's lack of response, and Tarah's disinterest, his life wasn't going at all as he had planned.

CHAPTER 10

After hours spent on his knees bombarding heaven with desperate questions, Anthony still had no answers. Releasing a weary breath, he wiped the tears from his cheeks and stretched out on his bed. He closed his eyes, but sleep eluded him as his mind whirled like a spring twister.

Two weeks had passed since the picnic, and whether Anthony liked it or not, Ben's words weighed heavily on his heart. His nerves were taut with uncertainty.

Conflicting thoughts warred against each other like two great armies on a field of battle. While he didn't want to neglect the salvation message, how could he ignore the spiritual needs of folks who were truly living for God? Should he abandon his firm message of the consequences of sin and begin to teach the fundamentals of godly living as Ben, in his innocence, had suggested?

It would have been so easy to disregard the boy's comments — and he had been prepared to do just that — but last week's message had once again fallen on deaf ears. The apathy on the faces of the few remaining members of his congregation had drained his enthusiasm for his message, and for the first time he doubted his mentor's teachings.

Were these people really hard-hearted and unwilling to hear the Bible preached? If so, why were several families still meeting at the Johnson farm on Sunday mornings to read scripture and sing hymns? Even Tucker, Anthony had heard, was beginning to attend the home group. His congregation was split in half, and Anthony felt the weight of responsibility for the division heavily upon his shoulders.

In preparation for today's sermon, he had prayed and studied the apostles' letters to the churches. Every one of them. But he hadn't received a clear answer. Services would begin in four hours, and he still had nothing to feed his sheep.

Frustrated, he pushed away the heavy quilt covering him and sat up on the edge of his bed. He swiped a hand through his hair and looked up as though the answers might be inscribed on the ceiling.

With his arms bent at the elbows, he held his hands palms up. "What is it, Lord? What am I doing wrong? If I am truly speaking Your message, then why have people stopped attending services?" In the early church, God had added souls daily. Even amid opposition to the apostles' teachings. So why was his church getting smaller and smaller?

With a resigned sigh, he dressed, grabbed his Bible from the table beside his bed, and tiptoed through the house. He snatched an apple from the kitchen table, shoved it into his coat pocket, then quietly exited the house, leaving the morning chores to his brothers.

He entered the schoolhouse in the darkness. After building a fire in the woodstove, he sank onto one of the wooden benches behind a desk. Weary from lack of sleep and spent tears, he leaned his elbows on the desk and stared into the darkness, wondering what he would say to his congregation when they arrived expecting a sermon.

"I guess I could give them an object lesson." He gave a short, bitter laugh. "The children sure loved it." As a matter of fact, his lesson to Tarah's class had garnered the only favorable response he'd received for his preaching since he'd moved back to Harper.

As light from the east filtered in through the window, slowly pushing the inky blackness from the room, so, too, did the fog begin to lift from Anthony's mind.

For the last few weeks, he had been preaching salvation to the saved. Redemption to the already redeemed. The time had come for a new approach.

Concern sifted over Tarah as Anthony walked to the pulpit, the usual spring in his step noticeably absent. Dark smudges appeared under his eyes, and his face was a full shade paler than normal. Clearing his throat, he paused and stared out over the congregation.

When his gaze met hers, he gave her a crooked grin, as though reassuring her. Tarah felt herself flush and quickly averted her gaze.

Though she had been furious with him for taking Louisa Thomas to the picnic, she'd found herself unable to hold a grudge — not after the way he'd defended, then gone after, Laney.

If he preferred Louisa, so be it. Though Tarah's heart couldn't help beating a staccato in his presence, she had resigned herself to his friendship.

"Let's begin with prayer," Anthony said, as he did each Sunday morning.

Tarah held her breath and nearly mouthed the words "Our most gracious heavenly Father" along with him.

"May your words pour like honey on the ears of the listeners today. And may the truth penetrate each heart and mind. In Jesus' name, amen."

Tarah lifted her head and opened her eyes, observing him with the same quiet surprise she was sure was reflected in each face present. Something was different.

Slowly Anthony reached inside his pocket and produced an apple. Then he pulled out a small knife, as well.

Feeling a hand on her arm, Tarah glanced down into Laney's questioning eyes. "How's he gonna preach if he's eatin'?" she whispered. "Yer ma says it ain't polite to talk with yer mouth full."

"It's not polite to talk during service, either," Tarah whispered back, placing a finger to the little girl's lips.

She couldn't imagine what Anthony was thinking, and she wondered if his pale countenance and the dark rings under his eyes were indications of an illness. Twisting around, she caught Dr. Simpson's gaze. He shrugged and sent her a reassuring smile, then glanced back up at Anthony, concern written on his leathery face.

Slowly Anthony sliced through the apple, then held up one half in each hand.

Shuffling noises could be heard throughout the room, and Tarah knew the bewildered congregation wondered if their preacher had suddenly gone daft.

Anthony sent a wry grin around the room. "Bear with me, folks. I'm not crazy yet."

Nervous laughter made its way through the smattering of people present, and Tarah felt some of the tension leave her shoulders.

"Now let me ask an obvious question. What kind of seeds would you say are inside here?"

"What kinda fool question is that?" Mr. Collins asked, earning him a firm elbow in his side from Mrs. Collins.

"It's all right, Mrs. Collins. Don't burn his dinner just to teach him a lesson. I did ask a silly question."

Mrs. Collins blushed as her husband chortled. "Thank you, Preacher," he said. "She just mighta done that."

Again the congregation rumbled with laughter.

A thrill passed over Tarah's heart as she sat watching Anthony speak as though he were passing the day in Tucker's store. For the first time ever, he was reaching his congregation.

"Even the youngest among us," Anthony continued, "understand that inside an apple are apple seeds."

He glanced around the room until his eyes lit on young Sally Hammond. "Sally, when your pa plants his hayseed, what grows?"

The little girl blushed and ducked her head. "Aw, Preacher, you know."

"Answer the man's question," Mr. Hammond said sternly.

"Yes, Pa."

Anthony's features softened. "What grows from hayseeds?"

"Hay," she whispered, her face glowing bright red.

"That's right. Even a child knows that you get what you plant."

He held up the apple once more. "Although you may not know how many apples come from one seed, you can be assured of the kind of fruit it will produce."

Tarah drew a breath and waited for him to come to the point.

"Galatians 6:7 says, 'Be not deceived; God is not mocked: for whatsoever a man soweth, that shall he also reap.' " He swallowed hard and walked around the pulpit to stand directly before the congregation.

"For the past few weeks, I've sown seeds of judgment and criticism to the folks in this town. The fruit I reaped from those seeds were criticism of my preaching and division among the good Christian folks of Harper."

Tarah's eyes moistened as his voice faltered, and she longed to throw her arms around him and reassure him. The silence in the room was deafening as the congregation watched. When he had composed himself, Anthony continued.

"There are only a few weeks left in my trial period. Lord willing, I will preach a series of messages on living a godly life." He swallowed hard. "To those of you who have come each week despite my shortcomings, I thank you for your support and prayers. And I'll do my best to make amends to the folks who felt they had to leave."

The sounds of sniffling filled the room as ladies placed handkerchiefs to their noses and men cleared their throats.

The sight of Anthony standing so vulnerable and open before his congregation tore at Tarah's heart.

"I know it's a mite early, but this is all the Lord placed on my heart to share."

Tarah smiled through tears as he said a

short closing prayer and moved down the aisle toward the doorway. She hung back, waiting for her chance to shake his hand.

Her pulse quickened at Anthony's bright smile as she approached.

"You did well," she murmured. He reached out and took her proffered hand, enveloping her with his warmth.

"Thank you, Tarah." His gaze penetrated her, snatching her breath away. "I was wondering —"

Tarah stumbled forward as a flash of blue taffeta and lace brushed past. Louisa claimed her place next to Anthony and clutched his arm possessively. "Oh, Anthony. You were simply wonderful."

Tarah resisted the urge to stomp her foot. Why did Louisa always have to show up and ruin everything?

"Thank you, Louisa," Anthony said, keeping his gaze fixed on Tarah.

Louisa followed his gaze, eyes narrowing dangerously. "Wasn't that just the most clever illustration you've ever seen, Tarah?"

"It was very inspired," she murmured, unable to break Anthony's hold on her.

Louisa's voice continued as though nothing were amiss. She tapped his arm with her closed fan. "I don't know what you meant by apologizing, though. You've always done a wonderful job. I think folks just don't appreciate you."

Anthony cleared his throat and turned his attention to Louisa, a look of faint amusement covering his face.

"If you'll excuse me," Tarah said.

"Wait." Anthony reached forward and placed a restraining hand on her arm.

"Oh, Anthony. Don't be rude," Louisa said, tightening her grip on his arm. "Tarah needs to join her family. See, they're all waiting in the wagon."

Anthony released his hold on Tarah's arm. "I guess it can wait," he mumbled.

Louisa gave a bright laugh that Tarah didn't quite believe. "Besides, I have our picnic all packed and ready to go."

A frown furrowed Anthony's brow as he turned back to Louisa. "Picnic?"

"Why, of course. We were interrupted last time." She glanced pointedly at Tarah. "And last week it was raining."

"Don't let me keep you from your picnic." Tarah sent Anthony and Louisa as bright a smile as she could muster and hoped they didn't notice the tremble of her lips. "Good day."

Without waiting for a response, she hurried to the wagon.

Tarah jammed the needle through the cloth and made yet another crooked stitch in the banner draped in a circle across four laps. Why she had to participate in making the decorations for the end-of-school dance just because she was the teacher, she'd never know. Sewing had always been somewhat of a mystery to her, despite Cassidy's attempts to help her learn.

Listening to Louisa prattle on about how excited she was that Anthony would be escorting her to the silly dance grated on Tarah's nerves like the sound of a squeaky wagon wheel. And the nods of approval from the two matrons present sent Tarah into a tizzy of emotions. She figured she must be the only person in Harper Township except Laney who could see right through Louisa's manipulations. To Tarah's way of thinking, there was nothing worse than knowing what a mistake Anthony was about to make and being unable to stop him without sounding like a jealous schoolgirl.

"Don't you think so, Tarah?"

Tarah started, jamming the needle painfully into her finger. She jerked her hand away, pulling the banner with her. As it bil-

201

lowed to the floor, she felt the disapproval from Louisa's mother. Heat crept to her cheeks, and she quickly snatched up her end of the material. "Sorry," she mumbled. "I — I pricked my finger."

"Well, whatever you do, don't get blood on the material," Louisa squealed. "It'll be ruined."

"Oh, honestly. It isn't bleeding that badly." Tarah hastened to assure the women, whose worried frowns revealed they weren't happy with the threat of being forced to remake the almost-finished banner. She grabbed her handkerchief from the reticule at her feet and wiped away the dot of blood on the tip of her finger, then resumed her sewing.

"Back to what I was saying," Louisa said, as though Tarah's finger weren't throbbing. "Don't you think so, Tarah?"

Oh, don't I think what? Tarah thought tersely.

She would have asked Louisa to repeat the question, but from the way the women stared at her, obviously awaiting her response, she couldn't bring herself to admit her mind had been a million miles away.

She cleared her throat and slid her tongue over her lips. "Yes, I suppose so," she murmured, returning her gaze to her crooked stitches.

"You see, I told you if anyone would know, it would be Tarah. Her pa being on the town council and all." The triumph in Louisa's voice caused Tarah's stomach to do a flip-flop.

What on earth had she just confirmed?

"Do you really think so, Tarah?" asked Louisa's ma. "It would be wonderful if Anthony were kept on as preacher after his trial is over. He's been preaching so beautifully the past few weeks. And now that everyone has started coming to services again, I'd be mighty surprised if the town council didn't approve him as the permanent preacher."

"Oh." How did they expect her to know whether Anthony was to be kept on or not? "It certainly would be wonderful. But I suppose we'll have to wait and see with everyone else."

"But I thought you just said he would be," Louisa challenged, her green eyes narrowing. "Really, Tarah, if you didn't know, you should have just said so."

"I–I'm sorry, I didn't mean to suggest I knew for sure."

"Of course you didn't," Hannah Simpson, the doctor's wife, said soothingly. "Tarah was speculating just like the rest of us."

Tarah could have kissed the woman. She

glanced up to give her a grateful smile and caught her breath at the look of sympathy in Hannah's eyes.

"Well," Louisa said haughtily. "One would certainly think the daughter of the most prominent member of the town council would know *something*. I certainly would if my father had ever been elected to the council."

Maybe your father would have been voted to the town council if he hadn't foreclosed on half of the farms in the township in the last four years. Tarah knew it was a sore topic for Louisa that her pa wasn't directly involved in the town business. But the banker was ruthless, she had heard her pa comment. Never once had he extended mercy. If a person was late on a payment, the bank took the land — lock, stock, and barrel.

Thankfully Pa had made a success of the St. John ranch before the area was heavily settled. He didn't have to rely on good crops to make ends meet, and as long as the cattle and horses did well at auction, the ranch thrived.

"My pa doesn't share town business with me, Louisa. And I wouldn't ask him to."

Louisa sniffed and resumed her delicate stitching. "Still, I'd find a way to make sure

Anthony was kept on. But I guess that's because he and I . . ." A delicate blush appeared on her cheeks as she slid her gaze to Tarah's. "Well, I suppose I shouldn't say anything yet. Anthony wants to wait until he knows for sure he has a way to support us."

"Why, Louisa." Mrs. Thomas stopped sewing and stared with delight at her daughter. "Why haven't you told me?"

"W—well," Louisa's voice faltered, and she glanced from Tarah to her mother. "We haven't made any firm plans yet."

Tarah felt the high collar of her gown choking her. Her throat went suddenly dry, her palms grew damp, and she was almost sure she felt a faint coming on. She stared dumbly at Louisa as her mother wrapped her arms around her and squealed gleefully.

"My baby, finally getting married. We'll have to order a copy of the latest *Godey's Lady's Book* to see what is in fashion for wedding gowns. And of course we must order the finest silk and lace from Paris." Her eyes widened with inspiration. "Your brother Caleb will be coming home from the university in a couple of weeks. Wouldn't it be wonderful if he stood up next to Anthony at the wedding?"

"Well, I don't know, Mother," Louisa

205

mumbled. "Anthony has brothers he might prefer."

Mrs. Thomas waved away Louisa's comment. "And, oh, Tarah," she babbled on, as though Tarah's heart weren't nearly breaking in two, "do you think Cassidy would be available to make the gown? She did such a fine job on Louisa's ball gown last year."

Choking back the tears, Tarah spoke around a lump in her throat. "Why, I don't know. Pa doesn't want her taking on too much with the new baby coming."

"Oh, well, we don't need to speak about such an indelicate topic, dear," Mrs. Thomas reproved. "I'm sure Cassidy would be appalled by your manners."

Mrs. Simpson chuckled. "Around a doctor's home, childbirth is hardly an indelicate subject."

Thankfully Mrs. Simpson had volunteered to head up the decorating committee.

Mrs. Thomas's lips thinned into a tight smile. "I never have quite gotten used to the crudities of life out here. In Charleston, we would never consider speaking of such things in the parlor."

"I do apologize, Mrs. Thomas," Tarah said. "I don't know what I was thinking to bring up such a subject."

Mollified, the older woman nodded and

gave a delicate wave of her hand. "Oh well. I suppose I should expect such manners from a young lady raised in these parts," she said charitably. "We can hardly fault you for your manners."

Tarah's temper flared. She opened her mouth to speak, but Mrs. Simpson spoke up first. "How about some coffee and apple pie, ladies? I think we're about finished for today. One more session, and the banner will be completed." She laid the banner aside with care and turned to Tarah. "Will you help me bring in the refreshments, Tarah, dear?"

Grateful for the opportunity to escape, Tarah lifted the banner from her lap and fairly bolted from the room.

Once inside the kitchen, Mrs. Simpson took hold of Tarah's arms and fixed her with a firm gaze.

"Now you listen to me, Tarah St. John. Don't let them make you feel like you're less than they are. You hear?"

Hot tears sprang to Tarah's eyes. Unable to utter a word, she nodded.

"You come from the finest family I know, or I wouldn't be allowing my Camilla to marry your brother, now, would I?"

"M–marry?" Tarah croaked.

Mrs. Simpson's eyes grew wide, and she

released Tarah's arms. "You mean you don't know?"

"Know what?" *Could this day bring any more bad news?* Surely Mrs. Simpson was speaking of the future when Sam and Camilla would inevitably become betrothed.

"Oh, honey. I can't believe they haven't told you yet. Your ma and pa gave their blessing a week ago."

"B–blessing?" she croaked. Panic welled up in Tarah, and dread knotted her stomach, making her suddenly ill. "Do you mean Sam and Camilla are . . . ?"

A worried frown creased Mrs. Simpson's brow. "It never occurred to me you didn't know. I can't imagine why . . ." She studied Tarah's face for a moment, then nodded. "You're in love with Anthony, aren't you?" Compassion filled her eyes. "I thought I saw it while we were sitting in there, but I wasn't sure."

Unable to deny the statement, Tarah sank into a kitchen chair and rested her chin glumly in her palm. "I guess my family didn't want to hurt me with the news my younger brother is getting married. Especially when the man I love is marrying someone else."

Mrs. Simpson snorted. "I wouldn't be too sure of that."

Tarah's gaze darted to the older woman. "What do you mean?"

"Well." She glanced toward the kitchen door and dropped her voice a notch. "I'm not one to gossip, but did you notice how quiet Louisa got when her ma started talking about ordering silk from Paris?"

Now that she mentioned it, Louisa had seemed a mite nervous.

"You see? You noticed it, too." Mrs. Simpson gave a quick nod and collected four plates, four cups, and a tray from the cabinet. She allowed Tarah to digest the hopeful news while she cut four generous slices of apple pie. "I'd bet my right arm Louisa was just trying to get under your skin and got herself dug into a hole instead." She gave a quick laugh. "I'd love to see her try to scratch her way out."

Tarah shrugged. "It doesn't matter. Eventually he'll ask her. And if I know Louisa, she'll make it happen pretty quickly now that her ma thinks she's already snagged him."

"If that day ever comes, I'll be the most surprised woman in Harper," Mrs. Simpson retorted. "I've watched him, and I'll tell you, our young preacher's in love. But not with Louisa."

Tarah groaned inwardly. Bad enough to

lose him to Louisa, but at least she could console herself that he was being fooled. What other woman could possibly have won his affections without Tarah's notice?

"You really don't see it, do you, honey?"

"See what, Mrs. Simpson?"

"Unless I miss my guess — and I rarely do — our preacher is head over heels in love with a certain Miss St. John."

"Oh, Mrs. Simpson, you don't have to say that. Anthony and I have become friends. But he's smitten with Louisa."

Lifting the tray, Mrs. Simpson sent Tarah a confident smile. "Mark my words. Anthony may not know it yet, but you're the woman for him. You just have to make him see it."

Tarah lifted her chin, remembering the humiliating experience of Anthony's amusement the one time she had attempted to flirt. "I won't resort to manipulating him like . . . well, like some people would. If Anthony can't see the truth, then that's his own misfortune."

Mrs. Simpson chuckled and walked to the door, then turned back to Tarah. "Anthony knows you're not like Louisa. But do you have to be as bristly as a cat getting ready to pounce all the time?" she whispered. "He's probably scared to death you'll scratch his eyes out if he ever speaks his mind." She opened the door before Tarah could reply.

"Now who's ready for some of my famous apple pie?"

CHAPTER 11

Anthony drove the last nail into place, then tested the shutter to see if it would swing properly.

"Ya did it, Preacher," Laney said, nodding in grudging approval. "Reckon Mr. Garner's gonna be mighty glad we come out here to fix up the mess my pa made of the place."

"Reckon so," Anthony replied. He knew Laney still thought he was courting Louisa, and it gave him no pleasure that he was unable to convince her otherwise. Even more embarrassing was the fact that this little urchin had doubts about his intelligence because of that belief.

"Me an' Ben finished puttin' all the junk in a pile. Can I light it on fire?"

"I think I'd better do that," Anthony said. "But you can pour the kerosene over the pile."

She brightened at the idea. "Can I do it now?"

"Yes, but don't try to light it."

Flashing a quick grin, Laney took off across the yard.

Anthony glanced through the open shutter at Tarah, who labored to clean up the filthy soddy. "How's it going in there?"

She looked up, a weary smile on her lips. "I should be finished sometime around Christmas, I figure."

"We're just about finished with the outside," he replied, chuckling at her remark. "Then we'll all come inside and pitch in."

"I'd welcome your help." Tarah planted her hands on her hips and scowled. "Honestly, Anthony. How can a man allow his home to become so filthy? I wouldn't let my favorite pig live in this place."

"Jenkins must have been mighty miserable. I pray he finds the Lord, wherever he ends up."

The scowl left Tarah's face, and she drew in a deep breath. "I suppose you're right. I've been awfully hard on him. I just can't seem to help myself. When I think of the treasure he possessed in those precious children, only to throw them away as if they meant nothing, it just makes me want to scream." She waved to emphasize her words, and her hand knocked against the kettle warming on the stove. A look of pain flickered across her face. Instantly Anthony sprang from his place at the window and ran into the soddy.

"Are you okay?" he asked.

She held on to her wrist and blew on an angry red mark already beginning to blister on the back of her hand. "I'm all right. This is my own fault for being so angry I wasn't paying attention to what I was doing."

"Here," Anthony said, "let me see it."

Offering her hand with the trust of a child, Tarah drew in her bottom lip.

"This is a pretty bad burn," Anthony observed, inwardly berating himself for distracting her in the first place. "We'd better get you home so you can tend to it."

"Honestly, it's just a silly little burn. I want to finish up here."

"No," he said firmly. "I'm taking you home right now. The cleaning will keep until another day."

Tarah's eyes grew stormy, and she narrowed her gaze. "What do you mean, no? If I want to stay and finish cleaning, I will."

In spite of himself, Anthony laughed outright. "Now you sound just like our little Laney. Who's teaching whom?"

A pretty blush rose to her cheeks, sending a rush of warmth to Anthony's heart. He loved this woman so much it hurt. But the knowledge that he rated only friendship in her heart made his stomach clench so tightly at times, he could barely stand the ache.

"Really, Anthony, it's nothing to be concerned about."

"It is something to be concerned about. You can't work in this filth with a blister on your hand. It could become infected."

Glaring at him, Tarah finally sighed in concession. "Oh, all right, but I think you're making a lot of noise over nothing."

"It isn't nothing to me, Tarah," he said. "I just don't want to see you sick."

All the thunder left her face as she met his gaze.

Still holding her hand, Anthony stepped closer. He brushed at a smudge on her cheek, marveling at the softness of her skin. "Tarah," he whispered, darting a glance to her slightly parted lips. Anthony's insides quivered as he drew her close. He longed to kiss away any thoughts of mere friendship from her mind and show her it was she, not Louisa Thomas, who held his heart. And heaven help him, he was getting ready to do just that.

"Just kiss her, would ya? Ya know ya want to."

Tarah gasped at the sound of Laney's

voice and quickly moved away. "No one was going to kiss anyone. I — I just hurt my hand, and Anthony was looking at it for me, Laney."

"That ain't the way it looked from where I'm standin'," Laney said with a snort. "So are we gonna light up that pile of junk out there, or ain't we, Preacher?"

"Like Tarah said, she hurt herself. We're going to take her home first. Then we'll come back and light the fire."

"Ya really hurt yerself?" Laney frowned and strode to Tarah's side. "Think we oughtta take her to the doc, Preacher?"

A tender smile curved Tarah's lips as she looked at Laney. "I'll be all right, honey. I just need to put some butter on it for the pain. Reverend Greene is afraid I might get it dirty, and that could make me sick."

Laney turned on Anthony. "What're ya doin' just standin' there? We gotta get Tarah home 'fore she gets sick." She hurried out the door. "Ben," she bellowed. "We're leavin'. Hurry up."

Shaking her head, Tarah gathered up her reticule. "I suppose I should be glad I have so many people to worry about me."

"People who love you," Anthony corrected.

Eyes wide, Tarah stared silently at him

until he felt himself blush beneath her questioning gaze.

He cleared his throat, ready to declare his love and take his chances.

"What are ya waitin' fer?" Laney stuck her head through the doorway, a scowl marring her features. "Do ya want Tarah to get sick?"

Sighing in frustration, Anthony took Tarah by the elbow and steered her toward the door. "If we don't get out to the wagon, that child is likely to try to carry you out there herself."

During the drive to the St. John ranch, Anthony watched for signs that Tarah had been moved as much as he during their closeness at the soddy. Disappointment crept through his gut as she talked and laughed with the children, looking as though the almost-kiss had never happened.

In view of her apparent lack of emotion, Anthony felt relief that he hadn't put his heart into her hands by telling her he loved her.

Help me to accept this, Lord.

If friendship was all this amazing woman had to offer, he would accept it, no matter how much it hurt. Her friendship was better than nothing at all.

■ ■ ■ ■

As the days grew shorter and the time grew closer for the school term to end, Tarah was filled with uncertainty. She had to give Mr. Halston an answer before Christmas so Starling's town council would have time to secure another teacher should Tarah decide not to accept the position. The school term was to begin in February, he informed her, and the schoolhouse now sat completed at the edge of the small town.

As the chilly autumn air gave way to a mid-November freeze, Tarah still hadn't made a decision.

Glancing out at her empty schoolroom, Tarah allowed her mind to imagine what it would be like to move away from home for a few months and teach a new group of students. Excitement warred with uncertainty, feelings all too common in the past few weeks.

Try as she might, she couldn't bring herself to heed Mrs. Simpson's advice and allow Anthony to see how deeply she cared for him. Fear wrapped around her heart each time she considered the possibility. It was just no use. Besides, the only time she saw him anymore was after service on

Sunday, and Louisa always claimed her place by his side, clinging to his arm with either a picnic lunch packed for the two of them or an invitation to her parents' house for dinner. Tarah held her breath each Sunday morning, praying Anthony wouldn't announce their betrothal from the pulpit. So far, he hadn't. But Tarah feared the day was fast approaching.

With a sigh, Tarah stood and began to tidy her small desk. Only two weeks remained in the school term. She had hoped by now that Anthony would have come to his senses like Mrs. Simpson believed he would. In her favorite daydream, she always penned a letter to Mr. Halston, thanking him for his patience but informing him she was to be married soon, so teaching in Starling was out of the question. So far, her dreams were only that: dreams. The wretched reality was that Anthony still seemed mesmerized by Louisa Thomas.

Gloomily Tarah gathered her belongings and headed down the aisle, just as Ben and Laney burst through the door. Pale and visibly shaken, their breath came in short, quick bursts.

A knot formed in Tarah's stomach at the fear widening each pair of eyes. "What is it?"

"W–we just seen Pa comin' out of Tucker's," Ben said.

Tarah gripped his shoulders and hurriedly scanned his face. "Ben, are you sure?"

"It were him, all right," Laney said, her lower lip trembling. "I ain't goin' back, and ain't nobody makin' me do it."

Ben limped to the window and peeked out. "Tarah, he's headin' over here. He musta seen us." Ben's voice shook with fear as he turned from the window. "We gonna have to go back?"

"I don't know, Ben." Helpless fury engulfed her at the thought of that man waltzing into town after weeks of abandonment and expecting to take the children back.

Over the past few weeks, Laney and Ben had lost the haunted expressions in their eyes. Now the hopelessness had returned.

"Well, you ain't just gonna let 'im take us back, are you, Tarah?" Laney's voice reflected her challenge, but her eyes held pleading.

Tarah lifted her chin, determination rising inside of her. "I'm going to do everything I can to keep him from it. You two go to the front of the room and stay by my desk while I speak with your pa."

Squaring her shoulders, Tarah moved toward the door, preparing for confrontation, praying for wisdom.

"Be careful, Tarah," Ben warned. "He can get downright mean if he's been drinkin'."

"Don't worry about me. I'll be fine." Tarah spoke with more confidence than she felt. Her insides quivered at the thought of confronting the man who had forced his children to live in squalor, practically starved them because of his laziness, and then abandoned them to the care of others. He was not worthy of his children, and she wouldn't let them go without a fight.

Oh, how she prayed God would make him see reason.

She drew a steadying breath, gathering her courage as the door swung open and Mr. Jenkins appeared at the threshold. He stared at her through narrow black eyes. "I heared you got my young'uns."

"Th–they've been staying at the ranch during your absence, yes."

"Well, I come fer 'em."

"I — I wanted to discuss that with you, Mr. Jenkins." Tarah motioned to a nearby desk. "Would you care to sit?"

"No, girlie, I don't wanna sit. I want my young'uns."

"But they've been so happy with us. They've even come to school and made friends." She looked into his unrelenting eyes and nearly sobbed. "Please let them stay."

He leaned toward her, his lips twisting into a sneer. Instinctively Tarah stepped back, despising her cowardice.

"So ya don' think I'm a fittin' pa, eh?"

"I didn't say that, Mr. Jenkins. But I — I know how much trouble you've had caring for them."

At the angry flush appearing in his cheeks, Tarah wished she could snatch the words back. The first unwritten rule in trying to get a man to see reason was to never wound his pride. And she had done just that.

"I'm sorry," she murmured. "I didn't mean to imply —"

"Where are they?" he demanded.

Couldn't the man see past the end of his nose? With a frown, Tarah turned toward the desk. A wave of relief swept over her. Laney and Ben were nowhere to be seen. "Wh–why, I don't know where they are," Tarah replied truthfully, though she had a feeling the pair was hiding under her desk.

"Well, I ain't a-gonna try and find 'em." He squinted his beady eyes and wagged a filthy finger inches from Tarah's nose. "Ya make sure them kids git their no-good hides to the soddy b'fore dark, or I'll be a-goin' to the sheriff."

He shuffled toward the door and slammed it shut behind him.

Weak with relief that the man was too lazy to look in the most logical hiding place available to the children, Tarah sank down in the nearest desk and glanced toward the front of the room. "You can come out now. He's gone."

The cloth covering her desk moved, and Laney and Ben crawled out.

Laney hopped to her feet and ran down the aisle. She hurled herself into Tarah's arms. "Don't let 'im take us back, Tarah. I promise I'll do chores w'thout complainin', and I won't trip Luke no more just 'cause he's walkin' by; and next time I pitch the baseball at recess, I won't throw it at that Josie Raney on purpose and try and hit her. A—and I can even say them words to Jesus, like Preacher wants me to." She gathered in a deep, shuddering breath. "I'd do anythin' to stay with ya."

Hot tears burned Tarah's eyes. She blinked them back and swallowed hard, holding Laney at arm's length. The tear-streaked face stared back at her with more vulnerability than Tarah had ever seen in the child.

"Let's go home and talk to my pa," she said when she recovered her voice. "If anyone can change your pa's mind, it'll be my pa."

"Do you really think he might wanna keep us, Tarah?" Ben's face lit with hope. "It's awfully crowded at yer place."

Tarah's lips curved into a soft smile. "Of course he'll want to keep you. You're part of the family now. Aren't you?"

"We are?" The expression on Laney's face mirrored her brother's. A mixture of disbelief and hope.

Gathering the child back into an embrace, Tarah brushed a gentle kiss on her head. "Of course you are."

"I — I love ya, Tarah."

"I love you, too, Laney." She glanced up at Ben over the little girl's head. "And you, too, Ben."

The boy's face glowed, and he looked away quickly, dashing a tear from his cheek.

Laney stepped out of Tarah's arms, a frown creasing her brow. "Aw, he ain't gonna give us up. Folks only give 'im charity 'cause of Ben and me."

Ben's face clouded over at his sister's words. "Laney's right. He ain't never gonna give us up. We'd better just git on home."

"But let's at least give it a try. Maybe my pa can convince him."

Shaking his head, Ben steered Laney

toward the door. "It ain't no use." He stopped before stepping outside and turned back to Tarah. "Ya been awful good to Laney and me," he said. "Nicer than anyone I can ever r'member, 'ceptin' our ma — but Laney don't r'member her."

Tears flowed down Tarah's cheeks at the hopelessness reflected in each face. "Can't you just wait? I'm sure my pa —"

"I figure it ain't right to ask yer pa to do that. 'Sides, don't that Bible say, 'Children, obey your parents, fer *this* is right'?"

"Well, yes, but, Ben —"

"Then this is the right thing fer us to do. It's better iffen we just head on home. And, Tarah, I'm askin' ya to promise me ya won't ask yer pa to come to the soddy."

"But —" Tarah stopped at Ben's pleading glance. She nodded. "I promise."

With his arm still firmly about Laney's shoulders, Ben steered her out the door and limped away. Tarah watched as the two bravely headed through the freshly fallen snow in the direction of the soddy. When they were out of sight, she pressed her hands to her face and wept.

The sound of thundering hooves accompanied the *thud* of Anthony's ax as he brought it down hard, splitting a log in two.

He straightened up and swiped an arm across his sweaty brow, glancing toward the cloud of dust headed in his direction. Recognizing Tarah, he dropped the ax and ran toward her, his heart hammering against his chest.

Abby skidded to a halt a mere foot from him. One glance at Tarah's tear-streaked face confirmed something was horribly wrong.

She slid into his outstretched arms and clung to him, babbling nonsensical words that were muffled by his shoulder. Heart in his throat, Anthony held her, stroking her hair while she sobbed. When the tears were spent, she pulled away until he held her at arm's length.

"What is it?" he asked and fished a handkerchief — which he'd started carrying after the first time she'd wept in his arms — from his shirt pocket. He pressed the cloth into her hands.

"Thank you," she said, lips trembling.

Anthony gathered her close to his side with one arm about her shoulders and steered her toward the house. When they reached the porch, he motioned for her to sit. She sank onto the step and twisted the handkerchief in her hands until her knuckles grew white.

Dropping next to her, Anthony waited while she drew a ragged breath, then spoke, her voice thick with tears. "Mr. Jenkins came back and took Ben and Laney away."

Dread engulfed Anthony. "When?"

"Just after school today."

"I thought we'd seen the last of Jenkins."

"So did I," Tarah replied glumly. She turned to him, her violet-colored eyes wide with fright. "What if he takes them away where we can't look out for them?"

"If the man has any sense at all, he won't go anywhere with winter setting in." Anthony wasn't at all sure Jenkins had a lick of sense, but it was the least he could say to try to relieve Tarah's fears. By the dubious expression on her face, Anthony knew she was thinking the same thing.

"That's not too reassuring, Anthony," she said.

"I know."

With a groan, she pressed her cheek against his shoulder. "What are we going to do?"

Anthony felt his senses reeling at the lavender scent of her hair and the sweet warmth of her cheek through his shirt. He drew a breath and exhaled slowly, willing the moment to last forever. "Have you spoken with your pa yet?" he asked, his voice a hoarse whisper.

He felt her shake her head. "Ben made me promise not to. I came straight here from school."

"Why would Ben make you promise such a thing?" Anthony asked, his heart soaring at the knowledge she had come to him for help.

A shrug lifted her slim shoulders. "He doesn't feel right putting Pa in that position. A–and he quoted the verse about children obeying their parents." She raised her head and captured his gaze. "Honestly, Anthony. Sometimes I think Ben is the oldest person I know."

"I know exactly what you mean. That boy is special. I wouldn't doubt it if he becomes a preacher someday." He slapped his thigh in a moment of decision. "I'm going to go talk to Jenkins."

"Oh, Anthony." Tarah smiled through her tears. "I hoped you would."

He regarded her warmly. "All you had to do was ask. I told you once before I'd do anything for you."

Twin pink spots appeared on her cheeks, and she pulled away, ducking her head. "You're a true friend. But this isn't for me." She stood and met his gaze, determination sparking in her eyes. "We have to do this for

Ben and Laney."

Anthony shot to his feet. "What do you mean 'we'?"

"I'm going with you, obviously."

"I don't think so, Tarah. No telling how Jenkins might react."

Planting her hands firmly on her hips, Tarah sized him up, ready for a fight. "If you're going, so am I, Anthony Greene. Those children are as dear to me as my own flesh and blood. If I had a husband, I'd adopt them as my own, so don't you dare try to stop me."

"I'll marry you," he drawled. He searched her face, trying to gauge her reaction. "Then we can adopt them together."

Tarah scowled. "Very amusing, but I'm sure Louisa Thomas would have plenty to say about that."

Anthony was about to set her straight about his lack of romantic feelings toward Louisa, but she gave him no chance to speak.

"And don't think you'll marry her and adopt them if their pa agrees to let them go. Laney doesn't care too much for Louisa. I doubt she would want to live with her."

"And no one's making her do anything she doesn't want to do." Anthony chuckled to hide the sting as the truth of Tarah's feelings rammed into his gut once again.

A smile lifted the edges of Tarah's lips. "She's so special. Ben, too." A look of urgency filled her eyes. "Let's get going, Anthony. I don't want them to have to spend one night under the same roof as that wretched man."

Anthony followed as she headed toward the barn, obviously intent on getting Dodger saddled.

"I'm still not crazy about their lack of respect for their pa," he said. "Even if he is a no-account."

Tarah sniffed and glanced back over her shoulder. "I think they showed a great amount of respect by going back to him. I wanted them to hide out at the ranch while Pa tried to talk Jenkins into letting them go."

Anthony grinned and shook his head. "The man who marries you will have his hands full. I'll pray for him."

Tarah threw him a cheeky grin. "And you proposed just five minutes ago. Bet you're glad I didn't take you seriously."

But I was serious. I'd marry you tomorrow if you'd have me. The words were on the tip of his tongue, but he bit them back just in time. Why humiliate himself any more than necessary? Besides, they had other things to attend to at the moment. *If it's Your will those children leave their pa, please give me the wisdom to know what to say.*

CHAPTER 12

Tarah's thoughts whirled with what-ifs as she and Anthony rode to the Jenkinses' in relative silence. What if Anthony had been serious and really wanted to marry her? What if Laney and Ben could be their very own children? Then a bleak thought entered her mind. What if Mr. Jenkins refused to let the children go?

Tarah stiffened as they approached the soddy. The door was already off its hinges, another tattered blanket hanging from the doorframe. Several bottles littered the yard. Tarah stared in disbelief and disgust. And the man had only been back for one day!

They reined in their horses and dismounted as Mr. Jenkins stepped through the doorway, his fingers wrapped firmly around a half-empty bottle.

Laney darted around her pa. A cautious smile lit her face. "Howdy, Tarah, Preacher."

Roughly grabbing her skinny arm, Jenkins

pulled her back toward the door. "Git inside, gal," he said. Lifting a booted foot, he kicked her backside, then stumbled against the outside wall.

"That does it, Anthony," Tarah hissed. "If he refuses to let me have Laney and Ben, we'll wait until he passes out drunk, then steal them away."

Anthony reached out and lightly pressed Tarah's shoulder. "Let me do the talking, all right?"

"All right, but if he doesn't listen, we're doing it my way. I couldn't live with myself if I left those children in that horrid man's clutches."

Anthony gathered in a deep breath and plastered a smile on his handsome face. "Afternoon, Jenkins. When did you get back in town? We've been wondering about you."

Tarah gaped. Why was Anthony bothering with small talk? *Get to the point,* she inwardly urged.

Mr. Jenkins snorted. "Been expectin' company. 'Course, I figgered it'd be her pa," he said, waving the bottle in Tarah's direction. "Yer wastin' yer time, Preacher. Them's my young'uns, and I don' aim to be givin' 'em away."

Tarah couldn't hold back. She shook off Anthony's restraining embrace and stepped forward. "Please, Mr. Jenkins. This is no life for Laney and Ben."

Tipping the bottle, Jenkins took a swig, then wiped his mouth with his sleeve. His lips twisted into a cruel sneer. "Yer kind," he spat. "All the time thinkin' yer so much better'n me. Always thinkin' I don' do right by my young'uns." His bold, dark gaze raked over her, and Tarah felt the urge to duck behind Anthony.

As if feeling her discomfort, Anthony drew her close to his side.

"You and folks jus' like ya, all the time comin' around in yer fancy clothes an' holier-'n-thou attitudes. Well, Teacher Lady, I don' need the likes a you a-tellin' me how to live."

Tarah's temper flared, and she stepped away from Anthony once again. She planted her feet to give herself courage and drew herself up as tall as she could. "Frankly, Mr. Jenkins," she said, meeting his steely gaze head-on, "it's immaterial to me how you live your life. You can drink yourself into a roaring drunk and stay there if you wish. But I love Laney and Ben a great deal. And if you care anything at all for them, you'll let me have them."

"I don' give nothin' away for free, girlie." He cocked his eyebrow. "Iffen you catch my meanin'."

Tarah gasped, and her mouth dropped. The scoundrel was offering to sell his own children! Disbelief quickly became revulsion at the very thought. Then elation set in. She mentally calculated the money she had saved from her two months of teaching. She still had most of it. Almost fifty dollars.

"And just how much do children go for these days, Mr. Jenkins?"

"Tarah!" Anthony grabbed her arm and pulled her back. He eyed Jenkins. "Are you seriously suggesting we buy your children from you?"

"Iffen ya want 'em, I expect to be paid fair and square."

Anthony's voice rose considerably. "Laney and Ben are not animals to be sold off. They're living human beings. How can you even suggest such a thing?"

"Take it or leave it, Preacher." He slurred his words, and Tarah knew they didn't have much time before he was too far gone to be reasonable.

Fists clenched, Anthony stepped forward. Tarah's eyes widened. She couldn't let the preacher get into a brawl with a drunken man. Even if Anthony could take him. She grabbed his arm to halt him.

"Will you excuse us for just a moment,

Mr. Jenkins?"

"Take yer time," he said and tipped the bottle again.

Tarah pulled Anthony back to the horses where they could speak in private.

His brown eyes blazed. "Forget it," he said. "We are *not* buying those beautiful children from that skunk. I've half a mind to go to the sheriff and have him arrested."

"He'd just deny it." Tarah grabbed on to Anthony's muscled arms. "Now you listen to me, Anthony Greene. As if he wasn't despicable enough, now we see how horrid he really is."

Anthony groaned. "Tarah . . ."

"He probably never thought of selling those children before. But we put the thought into his head by wanting to take them from him. What if he tries to sell them to someone else?" Tarah shuddered at the thought. "Someone who won't love them?"

A flicker of doubt appeared in Anthony's eyes, spurring Tarah to fight on. "Don't you see? We have no choice. I won't take a chance on losing them forever to who knows what kind of life."

Nodding, Anthony grabbed one of her hands and pulled her back to the soddy. Mr. Jenkins tossed the now-empty bottle aside and folded his arms across his sunken chest. "Well?"

"What are your terms?" Anthony asked.

Jenkins scratched at the gray stubble on his chin. "Let's see here. A hunnerd a head oughtta do it."

Tarah gasped, and her heart sank to her toes. "I only have fifty."

"Well then, girlie, ya got yerself a problem, dontcha? Guess iffen ya really wanted 'em, ya could come up with the price."

"The children are priceless, Mr. Jenkins, and I'd give my last cent to take them home with me. But I don't have two hundred dollars." Tarah caught Anthony's gaze. The sickened expression clouding his face dashed her hopes.

"I'm afraid two hundred dollars is out of the question," Anthony said. "I don't have much cash money. No more than twenty dollars. Will you take seventy?"

"Well now, don' see as how I could." Mr. Jenkins scanned the horizon over Anthony and Tarah's head. "Say, Preacher. That's a mighty fine animal ya got there. Might be we could work somethin' out."

"You want my horse?"

"I gotta have somethin' to git me where I'm goin'. That ol' nag up and died on me a couple weeks ago. 'Course, I'd a-be needin' the saddle, too."

Anthony swallowed hard and glanced at Dodger. He clenched his jaw and turned back to Jenkins. "That horse is easily worth two hundred dollars. We'll make it an even swap. Tarah gets the children, and I throw in the saddle."

Tears filled Tarah's eyes at the thought of the treasure Anthony was willing to give up for the children's sake. She wanted to protest, to tell him he couldn't give the scoundrel his beloved Dodger, but her mouth refused to open. And one look into Anthony's eyes confirmed her feelings. No price was too great.

"Do we have a deal, Jenkins?" Anthony asked, his voice curt, almost gruff.

"Well, I'm needin' some cash money."

Tarah dug quickly into her bag and pulled out ten dollars. "This is all I have with me. Ten dollars and the horse."

His eyes lit with greed, and he reached out eagerly.

Tarah snatched her hand back. "Not until I see those children safely on my horse."

A scowl darkened his features. "Ben! Laney! Git out here."

Laney appeared. Then Ben. Tarah gasped at the sight of the boy. A bruise marred his eye, and he limped with greater care than normal, holding his side.

"You want us, Pa?"

"Nah, I don' wantcha. The teacher here does." His lips twisted into a cruel smile. "I don' know why she'd want a couple a worthless young'uns like you two. But yer hers now."

"You mean yer givin' us away? Just like that?" Laney's brow furrowed, her eyes filled with confusion.

"Go on. Git outta here," Jenkins bellowed. "An' don' bother to come back, 'cause I won' be here."

Hurt and anger flashed in Laney's eyes. She placed an arm around Ben's shoulder. "Come on, Ben. We don't stay where we ain't wanted."

Ben shrugged off her arm. "I don't need yer help."

"Fine," she shot back. "Fall on yer face, and see if I care!" But Tarah observed that she didn't leave his side.

Anthony strode to his horse. His hand curled around the leather reins, and he patted the black neck, whispering into Dodger's ear. Tarah watched as he gathered in a slow breath and handed over the reins.

"Laney, go climb up onto Abby." She slid her gaze to Ben. "Can you make it up, or should Anthony help you?"

Ben's soulful eyes stared back at her. "What about you? It's a good five miles to the ranch."

Tarah gave him what she hoped was a reassuring smile. "The walk will do me good. I've grown soft sitting in that schoolroom all day for the last two months. Come on now. Let's hurry." *Before he changes his mind.* "Can you make it up on your own?"

Ben nodded, seeming to understand.

When the children's backs were turned, Tarah hurriedly slipped Jenkins the ten dollars and spun around to join Laney and Ben.

Jenkins chuckled to himself, but no further words were spoken.

Squaring his shoulders, Anthony fell into step beside Tarah, and with the children on Abby, they headed for the St. John ranch.

In a bold move, Tarah grabbed Anthony's hand to comfort him. He laced his fingers with hers and held tightly, as though drawing on her for strength.

"I cain't believe Pa just up and gave us away," Laney said hotly.

The relief Tarah had expected from the children was replaced by the reality of indignation and hurt, emotions she had never expected from them.

"He ain't givin' us away, Laney," Ben said with a scowl.

"Do ya think I'm dumb? I got ears. Pa said we was Tarah's now. If that ain't givin' a person away, I don't rightly know what is."

"Pa sold us," he said curtly.

"Yer crazy," Laney retorted.

"Why do ya think Anthony and Tarah's walkin'? Pa got ol' Dodger, and I seen Tarah give 'im some cash money, too."

Laney's mouth dropped open, and she regarded Tarah and Anthony with disbelief. "You mean, you bought me and Ben like we was slaves?"

"No, sweetie," Tarah said. "We did what we had to do so you don't have to go back to your pa."

"Ya said we was like family," Laney said bitterly. "But we ain't. We're just slaves, bought and paid fer."

Tarah grabbed the reins and halted Abby. She laid her palm on Laney's jean-clad knee and met her accusing glare.

"You know Cassidy isn't my blood ma, right? And Emily isn't my blood sister?"

Laney nodded.

"But I love them as dearly as if they were blood kin. And Hope and Will are no less my brother and sister than Luke and Sam and Jack and Emily," she said, giving Laney a gentle smile. "It doesn't matter how you become a family. All that matters is that you love one another."

To Tarah's relief, Laney's face softened reflectively.

"And you really can keep us always?"

"Always."

Laney inclined her head. "Then I reckon we oughtta be gettin' home b'fore yer ma starts worryin'."

Anthony's wide smile greeted Tarah as she dismounted Abby two days later. He strode toward her from the front porch of his house, curiosity filling his brown eyes.

He gestured toward the other horse she led. "What's this?"

Tarah sent him a cheeky grin. "This, Anthony, is what is commonly referred to as a horse."

"You don't say," he drawled, patting the mare's chestnut neck. "She's a beauty."

"I'm glad you think so." Tarah could barely contain her excitement as she presented the gift to Anthony. "She's yours."

Accepting the reins with reluctance, Anthony's brow furrowed. "Mine?"

"My pa sent her over — our way of saying thanks for what you did for Ben and Laney."

"This isn't necessary, Tarah. I figure after next harvest I can get another riding horse.

In the meantime, there's always the wagon horses."

"You don't like her?" Tarah asked, disappointment reaching to her toes. "Pa said you can pick out another one if you prefer, but I thought you'd like this one the best. I know she can't replace Dodger. . . ."

The gentle caress of Anthony's finger upon her lips silenced her. "I didn't say I don't like her."

Trying to calm her racing pulse at Anthony's touch, Tarah stepped back, causing his hand to drop. "Then why not take her?"

"Would it mean so much to you?" he asked, his gaze searching her face.

She nodded, unable to find her voice.

A gentle smile lifted the corners of his mouth. "Then tell your pa I accept."

"Wonderful. He'll be pleased."

"How are Ben and Laney getting along?" Anthony asked, tethering the new mare to the rail spanning the length of the porch.

Tarah wrapped Abby's reins around the porch railing as well, then turned to Anthony. "They're doing wonderfully. Though Luke and Laney fight like a couple of wild dogs over a piece of meat." Tarah shook her head. "Honestly, Anthony. If it isn't one thing, it's another. And Luke is acting up in school again, too. I was afraid the reprieve was too good to last."

"And Jo?" He leaned against the rail and folded his arms across his broad chest.

Tarah hated to be a tattletale, but neither could she look Anthony in the face and lie. "Well, they aren't as bad as they used to be," she said, trying to sound nonchalant. "I suppose I can put up with them for a couple more weeks."

"I can speak to her ma about her."

Tarah shook her head. "Don't, Anthony. Your sister doesn't need to be upset in her delicate . . . well, you know."

A flush reddened Anthony's neck and cheeks, and he reached out, absently patting his new horse. Silence loomed between them momentarily until Anthony spoke. "Have you decided whether or not to accept the teaching position in Starling?"

Studying his face for any signs that he might want her to stay, Tarah felt her stomach drop as his eyes reflected only interest. No worry, no dread. Just interest.

She shrugged. "I haven't replied just yet. I have a few more weeks, but I suppose I'll go. The town council in Harper offered me another certificate for next term. So teaching in Starling will pass the time."

A heavy sigh escaped Anthony's lips. "So you won't be gone for good."

Tarah frowned, not sure if Anthony's sigh meant he was glad or disappointed that she'd be back. "No. Pa said the council is close to approving a full school term like in the cities, so once I'm back, I suppose I'll teach for as long as they'll have me."

"How do you think Laney's going to take the news you're going to Starling for five months?" Anthony sent her a crooked grin.

"I'll take Laney and Ben with me, of course," Tarah replied without hesitation.

Anthony's eyes widened. "You will?"

"I've already spoken to Pa and Ma about it. Laney and Ben are my responsibility, and I love them dearly. I want to take care of them." Tarah shifted her weight and regarded Anthony frankly. "I've spoken to Pa and asked him to consider building a small teacherage in town where the three of us could live once we return to Harper."

"And he agreed to that?" Anthony asked incredulously.

"He's agreed to speak with the council about it." Tarah's eyes narrowed. "Why shouldn't he?"

A shrug lifted Anthony's shoulders. "You're mighty young and, well, small to be taking on a ready-made family, don't you think?"

Tarah bristled and folded her arms across

her chest. "If I thought so, I wouldn't be doing it. And what does being small have to do with raising a couple of kids?"

"I don't know." Anthony raked his fingers through his thick hair and scowled. "Why do you have to get so riled up about things?"

"I don't know!" Tarah stomped to the railing and untied Abby just as the door swung open.

Anthony's gray-haired mother appeared at the threshold. "Where are you going, Tarah?"

"I was about to go home."

"Her pa sent me a horse," Anthony said sheepishly.

"How kind of him." A broad smile split her plump face, and she gave a cursory nod toward the new animal. "It's lovely. Anthony, have you forgotten we have a guest for dinner?"

Anthony's ears turned red. "I suppose I did."

"Well, you've left her to us long enough. You'd better get back inside." She turned to Tarah. "Honey, tie that horse back up and come on in. Your ma will know you're taking supper with us."

"Oh no. I couldn't intrude. Really. Especially if you have a guest." And especially if that guest was who Tarah had a feeling it might be. The thought of watching Louisa Thomas fawn all over Anthony through dinner not only robbed Tarah of her appetite — the unwelcome image made her positively ill.

Mrs. Greene waved away her protest. "Nonsense. There's always plenty in this house," she insisted. "And you haven't been out here since Anthony and Ella came back from the East. Anthony, tie up Tarah's horse, and both of you come in to supper." With that, she returned inside and let the door swing shut behind her, leaving no room for more argument.

Tarah glanced helplessly at Anthony.

"Ma doesn't take no for an answer," he said with an uneasy grin. "You'd better do as she says."

"Oh, all right."

Anthony cleared his throat as they walked together up the steps. "Tarah, there's something you should know about our dinner guest."

"Louisa?"

His Adam's apple bobbed as it always did when he was nervous, a habit Tarah found endearing, even now. He nodded. "I'm sorry. She just dropped by to bring Ma some quilting patches. And you know Ma. . . ."

"She can't help but take in wandering females?" Tarah gave him her best forced smile. "Don't worry, Anthony. I can be civil to your young lady for a couple of hours if I have to." She brushed past him and, without waiting for him to open the door, slipped inside, trying to choke back her humiliation.

Louisa's icy smile greeted them. "Why, Tarah, how lovely you dropped by — just at suppertime."

Heat rose to Tarah's cheeks at the implication.

"Tarah knows she's always a more-than-welcome guest in this house," Mrs. Greene said, giving Tarah a pat on the arm.

Louisa's nervous laughter filled the air, ringing Tarah's ears. "Well, of course she is. In every town the schoolteacher and the preacher are fixtures at one table or another, aren't they?"

"And even more so when they happen to be cherished friends," Mrs. Greene shot back.

Tarah looked between the two women, wondering if either realized what the exchange sounded like. From the embarrassed look on Ella's and Anthony's faces, she had a feeling she wasn't the only person in the room who recognized Anthony's mother as her champion. Unbidden sympathy welled within her at Louisa's red face.

Anthony held out Tarah's chair for her, and she sat gratefully, knowing her trembling legs would give out at any moment if forced to continue standing.

Rounding the table, Anthony took a seat next to Louisa. The smug smile curving Louisa's mouth said clearly, *I belong here, and you don't.*

Tarah kept silent during the meal, speaking only when spoken to. She fought to maintain her composure amid the humiliating experience and longed for the last bite of dessert when she could be on her way.

Louisa's incessant chatter grated on Tarah's already taut nerves until she wanted to cover her ears and scream.

"Tarah brought Anthony a beautiful mare from her pa," Mrs. Greene said during a pause in Louisa's prattle.

"Oh, you're buying a horse from the St. Johns, Anthony?" Louisa asked, a frown creasing her otherwise flawless skin. "I'm sure you could have gotten a better price in Abilene."

What does Louisa Thomas know about the price of horses? Tarah thought, defenses rising at the possible slight to her father's pricing of their animals.

"The St. John ranch has the finest reputation for quality stock around," Anthony said, his voice tense. "At an auction I wouldn't know what I was getting. Besides, I couldn't have asked for a better price. The horse was a gift."

"A gift?" Louisa's gaze riveted on Tarah, her eyes narrowing to two green slits, reminding Tarah of blades of grass peeking through the slats in the outhouse wall.

"My pa gave him the horse because of —"

"Because I lost Dodger," Anthony broke in.

Eyes widening, Tarah stared at Anthony. He hadn't told Louisa about Mr. Jenkins?

Seemingly oblivious to the exchange, Louisa pressed on. "Oh well, Anthony. I'm sure my father would be more than happy to buy you the finest horse in the state. Do be sensible and tell Mr. St. John you can't accept his gift."

Anthony's lips twitched. "Thanks all the same, but I believe I already have the finest horse in the state. And I'm not about to part with her."

He smiled at Tarah, sending her heart into a flutter.

"All right, Anthony, you keep whatever horse you want," Louisa said, placing a slender hand upon his arm. She glanced around the table. "I'd much rather talk about the dance anyway. Of course, your country dances are nothing like the balls I attended when we lived in Charleston, but these little diversions every now and then do tend to break up the dreariness of life out here." She turned to Ella. "I'm sure Tarah doesn't know what I mean, having lived here her whole life, but you certainly do, don't you?"

Ella sent her a kind smile. "We rarely attend fine balls, Louisa. I suppose we're just country folk at heart. I am greatly looking forward to the dance. I only wish my Joe were here."

"Uncle Anthony will dance with you, Ma," Josie piped in.

"You can d–d–dance w–w–with m–m–me, Ma," Toby said, regarding his mother with wide, adoring eyes.

Ella's face softened considerably. "Thank you, darlings," she said. "And just two days after the dance, we'll all go home to your father."

Mrs. Greene cleared her throat and stood. "Well then," she said, her voice faltering slightly. "Who's ready for dessert?"

Tarah's heart went out to Mrs. Greene, knowing how much she would miss her daughter and grandchildren when they returned to the East. "May I help you bring in the dessert, Mrs. Greene?"

Louisa shot to her feet. "Of course, where are my manners? Do let me help you."

The older woman gave a smile to include them both. "You two girls sit here and enjoy the conversation. You're guests, after all."

Louisa sat gracefully back into her chair.

Tarah stood. "I insist," she said, noting the mist forming in the older woman's eyes.

Once they reached the kitchen, Tarah lovingly reached out to comfort the older woman. "I know you'll miss Ella and the children dreadfully, Mrs. Greene. I remember how it nearly broke my granny's heart every day thinking of my aunt Olive not being nearby. Now that she's been visiting Aunt Olive for a few months, she misses us dreadfully and can't wait to return."

"I suppose when your children are grown, it's too much to hope they'll all stay close to home." Mrs. Greene wiped her eyes with the edge of her apron and smiled at Tarah. "I promised myself I wouldn't cry until Ella and the children were gone. But I suppose when the tears need to come, they just do, and there's nothing a body can do about it."

"No one expects you to be strong. And as happy as Ella is to be going home to her husband, I'm sure she'll shed a few tears of her own when the time comes to leave her ma."

Reaching up, Mrs. Greene pressed a hand to Tarah's cheek. "Such a good girl. Any mother would be proud to have you for a . . . daughter."

The kitchen door swung open, and Louisa burst in. "I thought I'd come and help, too."

"Thank you, dear." Mrs. Greene stepped back and moved to the counter.

Once Mrs. Greene's back was turned, Louisa threw Tarah a scathing look. Leaning in close, she whispered, "I know you're trying to make me look foolish, but it's not going to work. If all goes as planned, Anthony and I will have an announcement to make at the dance."

Before Tarah could respond, Louisa stepped forward. "Let me take that tray for you, Mrs. Greene."

"Thank you, Louisa. That's very sweet."

Louisa beamed. "Oh, I just love doing domestic things. I rarely have the chance at home, what with having Rosa to take care of menial tasks. You know, Rosa has been with our family ever since I can remember. Of course, we pay her now since we lost the war, but she doesn't try to throw that in our faces one bit."

Tarah released an exasperated sigh, then glanced quickly to see if the other two women had noticed. She found Mrs. Greene's gaze studying Louisa, a worried frown etching her brow.

"Well now. Let's not keep my family waiting on their dessert," she said, opening the kitchen door ahead of Louisa. Tarah trailed behind, wondering again what in the world Anthony saw in Louisa Thomas.

CHAPTER 13

In the light of the full moon, Anthony watched wistfully as Tarah headed off toward the St. John ranch with his brother Blane as her escort. He climbed into his saddle and smiled as best he could at Louisa, who sat astride her own mount. "All set?"

Louisa eyed his horse dubiously and nodded, nudging her mount forward. "I know you were trying to be polite, Anthony. But I really think you could find a higher-quality animal."

Irritation rose in Anthony. "I'm happy with this one, Louisa, but thank you for the offer."

"Oh well, let's not talk about that now anyway," she said brightly. "I'd much rather discuss the dance. I'll be the envy of all the girls, walking in on the arm of the most handsome man in town."

Anthony felt the heat rush up his neck and

burn his ears. He still wasn't quite sure how Louisa had finagled the invitation from him, but he'd regretted it ever since. Still, she deserved to have a nice evening. And maybe — if God allowed him — he could snatch one dance with Tarah. Preferably a waltz.

As if reading his thoughts, Louisa released a regretful sigh. "It really is a shame Tarah doesn't have an escort. I suppose I could ask my brother, Caleb, to invite her. Although she isn't really the elegant sort of young lady he normally courts. And there is also Tom."

"Tom?"

"A friend of Cal's. He accompanied my brother home from the university. He's even considering setting up a law practice in Harper, what with all the new people settling in the area. Of course, I don't see how he'll make the sort of living he could make in a city, but that doesn't seem to concern him a bit." Louisa paused to take a breath, then continued on as though speaking to herself. "Yes, I believe I'll suggest Tom invite Tarah to the dance. He's rather handsome. I suppose Tarah will be quite taken with him. I'll have to warn him not to give her any false hope. B–because, Anthony, there is nothing worse to a girl than receiving false hope from a man she fancies."

The way her voice faltered brought Anthony up short. He had supposed she had no idea how he felt. He'd taken great pains not to hurt her feelings over the past couple of months, but now he realized he had done her no favors by not being firm and refusing invitations. And furthermore, she was aware that he had been doing just that.

Taking a deep breath, Anthony sent up a silent prayer. "Louisa . . ."

The ring of false laughter filled the air as Louisa nudged her horse closer and reached out to place a hand on Anthony's arm. "Father just said this morning that he would be asking your intentions soon if you don't speak up. But I — I assured him you are too fine a man to trifle with a girl's affections. Aren't you, Anthony?"

The cautious hesitancy in her voice fanned Anthony's feelings of guilt, and he swallowed hard past the lump forming in his throat. Louisa might be flighty and annoying at times, but this new show of vulnerability sent a wave of compassion through Anthony. The time had come to stop the charade before she was hurt any more than she inevitably would be now.

"Stop for a minute, Louisa," he said, reining in his horse.

She did as he asked, and in the brightly lit night, Anthony saw the tears shimmering in her eyes. Her lips trembled as she stared back at him, a look of dread covering her delicate features. "Oh, Anthony," she whispered. "Please don't say it."

"I'm sorry," he mumbled. "I never should have led you on the way I did when I'm in love with —"

"Tarah," she said bitterly.

"Yes."

"Then why, Anthony?" she said, her voice thick with tears. "Why did you take me on picnics and ask me to the dance?"

What could he say without humiliating her? He had never asked her to go one place with him. He had even tried to refuse invitations from her, but she wouldn't take no for an answer. "I suppose I've been a cad, Louisa. I hope you'll forgive me."

"I don't know, Anthony," she said stiffly, jerking her reins and nudging her horse forward once again. "After all, you did lead me on. You aren't going to back out on escorting me to the dance, are you? Why, I'd be the laughingstock of the entire town."

Relieved that indignation had replaced the tears, Anthony smiled into the darkness and followed her. "I'm not backing out on the dance."

"That's little comfort for the humiliation I'll endure when the whole town finds out you preferred that mousy little country schoolmarm to me," Louisa huffed. "But it's better than the alternative."

The thought of his beautiful Tarah as a mousy little country schoolmarm brought a sudden smile to Anthony's face. Spunky, tenderhearted, and generous were traits that came to mind. He prayed she would hold off on answering Mr. Halston until after the dance so he could speak his heart freely. If only she shared a portion of his feelings, there was hope.

Dear Mr. Halston,

I am pleased to inform you of my recent decision to accept the teaching position you have so graciously offered to me. I will make arrangements to travel to Starling shortly after the New Year. Further correspondence will follow to inform you of the specific date of my arrival.

Sincerely,
Miss Tarah St. John

Tears blurred the words on the page as Tarah attempted to reread the letter. Once this was posted, there would be no turning back. She hadn't informed the family of her decision because she had just decided this very night to accept the teaching position. Louisa's presence at Anthony's house had proven she was holding on to a foolish dream.

Her heartbreak knew no bounds, but she couldn't be angry with Anthony. She loved him too much, and his happiness meant the world to her. But neither could she stay and watch as he became another woman's husband.

A soft rap sounded on her door. "Come in," Tarah said, tears thick in her voice. She tried to compose herself as Cassidy stepped into the room.

"I wanted to say good night."

Tarah nodded, afraid to trust her voice.

"Tarah?" Cassidy stepped closer. Cupping Tarah's chin, she inched her head up until they met eye to eye. "What's wrong?"

Hot tears sprang to Tarah's eyes, and she handed Cassidy her letter to Mr. Halston.

A troubled frown creased Cassidy's brow as she read. Gathering a deep breath, she gave the letter back to Tarah and sank down on the bed next to her. "I see you've made your decision."

"Yes."

"You'll need to tell your pa soon."

"I will." Tarah sniffed and brushed away a trail of tears with her fingertips.

"You don't seem very happy with your decision," Cassidy said, her eyes searching Tarah's face. "Are you sure you want to do this?"

A shrug lifted Tarah's shoulders. "I don't have a choice. Anthony is going to marry Louisa." With that she threw herself into Cassidy's arms and sobbed.

"Oh, Tarah, I'm so sorry. When did they make their announcement?"

"Huh?" Tarah pulled back and stared at her stepmother.

"Their betrothal announcement. When did they make it? I hadn't heard."

"Oh," Tarah said, waving a hand in dismissal. "They haven't yet. But it's only a matter of time."

"I see."

But Tarah could tell from the confusion on Cassidy's face that she didn't see at all. "I just can't stay here and watch Anthony marry her!"

"Are you sure this is what God wants you to do, Tarah?"

"I — I don't guess I've really prayed about it, Ma. I've been waiting to see . . ."

Cassidy drew an exasperated breath and planted her hands firmly on her hips. "Do you mean to tell me you are running off twenty miles from home just because the man you love doesn't love you in return?"

When she puts it that way . . .

Still, Tarah felt her defenses rise. Her life had been perfectly wretched the last few months. Between Luke and Jo making trouble in class, Anthony's love for Louisa, and Louisa always rubbing her nose in it, she needed to make a fresh start to regain her shattered dignity. And Starling was as good a place as any to do it.

Cassidy stood. "Honey, there's not a lot I can say. You have to make this decision for yourself, but running away is never the answer. If Anthony isn't the man God has for you, then He's preparing someone else. One decision has nothing to do with the other."

She strode toward the door, then hesitated. "Just make sure it's His will before you run off half-cocked because of your wounded pride. I'd hate to see you do something you'll regret later on."

Tarah said nothing as Cassidy slipped from the room, leaving her to wrestle with her words. Wounded pride, was it? She jerked her chin, then her shoulders slumped as truth rushed in like a raging tide. Was it wounded pride? She groaned aloud. Of course that's what it was. She loved Anthony, but he loved Louisa, a woman who clearly didn't understand or deserve him. Yet she, Tarah St. John, would have been the perfect wife for a man in his position. Thinking back, she remembered how her determination to love Johnny Cooper had almost killed her, Cassidy, and the twins.

Oh, God, I thought I had learned my lesson back then. Will I ever learn to trust Your will even when the answer is no?

Stretching out fully on her bed, she rolled to her stomach and allowed the tears to flow unchecked as she let go of Anthony, the most precious dream she had ever held in her heart.

In a flash, Cassidy's words from weeks before came back: *"Often the way we react to pressure shows us more about our own hearts than we would ever learn if things always worked out smoothly for us."* Her mind replayed every encounter she'd had with Louisa Thomas over the past few months since Anthony's arrival in Harper, and she saw how bitter and jealous she had become, growing more so with each meeting.

God, she prayed, *I was so sure You'd sent Anthony back here for me. But all the time he was only a test to see how I would react to his taking up with Louisa again.* And she had failed the test miserably. Her resentment toward Louisa had only hardened her heart. Sobs of repentance shook her body. *Mold me, like a potter molds clay, Lord. And please teach me to accept Your will for my life instead of always trying to manipulate my own course.*

Suddenly Tarah thought of the letter on her night table, and she sat up. All the weeks of indecision seemed to fade away, and she realized Cassidy was right. Her decision to leave was based on a desire to run away.

Even if she went to Starling, she would have to face Anthony and Louisa when she returned. And the thought of uprooting Laney and Ben didn't sit too well with her. They loved the family life she had always taken for granted. The more she thought about it, the more Tarah recognized that she wasn't ready to make such a drastic move either. Even if the town council approved the building of the teacherage, she would have months to prepare to set up housekeeping on her own. If she tried to do that now, she would be completely unprepared.

She stared at the letter for a moment longer, then knew what she had to do. She snatched it up and ripped it into pieces, feeling the pressure loosen in her chest with each tear.

Drawing a long, cleansing breath, Tarah stretched back out on her bed. She would stay in Harper and learn to get along with Louisa. Even now her bitterness toward the woman was abating, and she knew God would somehow take care of the rest. Her strong love for Anthony concerned her, but she felt confident God would take care of that as well. And if God willed her to fall in love again, He would send her a man who would return her love. But until then, she would keep her hands off God's business and trust Him to know what was best for her.

CHAPTER 14

Tarah hesitated at the double-doored entrance to the crowded livery stable, which had been transformed for the dance.

"Coming, Tarah?" Pa asked, holding out his arm. Cassidy looked radiant at his other side, dressed in a slightly snug gown of cream-colored satin.

"How could I resist being escorted by the most handsome man at the dance?" Tarah said, slipping her gloved hand inside the crook of his arm.

"Then let's make our grand entrance." Pa grinned to include Laney and Emily, who each held on to one of the twins. "I'm the luckiest man at the dance with all these beautiful women in my company."

Tarah had to admit they were a handsome group. Even Laney had acquiesced to wearing a dress, but she had made it clearly understood this was not to be an everyday occurrence.

Tarah grinned. Wearing a gown of blue velvet fashioned from material Cassidy had insisted was made just for Tarah, she felt confident in her appearance. But only for a moment. As she stepped inside, she spotted Louisa whirling past in Anthony's arms. Her gown of emerald-colored silk clung to her body and perfectly offset her green eyes, pale skin, and strawberry blond hair. Tarah had to admit, Louisa was breathtakingly beautiful, and suddenly she felt dowdy by comparison.

Anthony looked handsome in his Sunday suit and his tie, crooked as ever. Tarah couldn't keep an indulgent smile from curving her lips, though her heart ached at the sight of him dancing with Louisa.

She had barely removed her wraps when she was asked to dance. The evening whirled by with partner after partner vying for her attention until her self-confidence returned and she felt like the belle of the ball. She would have been on a cloud if only Anthony had once asked her to dance. But she knew it was just as well.

Standing next to the refreshment table, Tarah graciously refused a would-be dance partner and sipped a glass of lemonade, wishing she had brought a fan to cool herself off.

"Good evening, Tarah. Lovely dance, isn't it?" Louisa's singsong voice tore Tarah's attention away from watching Anthony waltzing with pretty Camilla Simpson.

In no mood for a confrontation, Tarah eyed Louisa cautiously, her stomach tense, awaiting the insults. But for once, the young woman smiled pleasantly. "I've made a decision, Tarah," she said, graciously accepting a glass of lemonade.

"Oh?" *Do you want me to be a bridesmaid?* Feeling a twinge of conscience, Tarah sent up a hasty prayer of repentance.

"Yes, I've decided Anthony is not the man for me after all. So you can have him."

Tarah felt her mouth drop at the sudden revelation. "What do you mean?"

With her gaze fixed on the dancers, Louisa inclined her head toward a young man Tarah had danced with earlier in the evening. "That's Tom Kirkpatrick, a friend of my brother's from the university." She cut her gaze to Tarah, apparently expecting a response.

"Handsome," Tarah obliged.

"Yes, isn't he?" Twin spots of pink dotted Louisa's cheeks. "We have discovered we have ever so much in common, and Mother and Father agree Tom is more suited to me than Anthony could possibly ever be."

Poor Anthony! "But what about your betrothal?" Tarah asked indignantly. "You can't just throw Anthony over for another man. It isn't right."

Louisa shrugged as she caught Tom's eye. The two shared a smile. "Better I find out now than after we're married. Don't you think?"

Tarah's temper flared. "I don't see how you can do this to Anthony after all this time of making him believe you would welcome a proposal."

Giving Tarah her full attention, Louisa lifted a delicate brow and regarded her reflectively. "I rather thought the news would please you. It's no secret how you feel about Anthony."

Heat rushed to Tarah's cheeks, but she met Louisa's gaze head-on. "How I feel isn't the point," she said, not caring that she had just made an admission. "Anthony's feelings are all that matter right now. And he'll be so hurt."

An amused smile played at the corners of Louisa's lips. "A bright girl like you should be able to find a way to help him feel better." She let out a short, mirthless laugh. "In fact, I wouldn't be surprised if he turns to you before the evening is over."

A retort fell short of Tarah's lips as her pa

stood on the rough-hewn platform at the front of the room and held up his arms. "Ladies and gentlemen, may I have your attention, please?"

The room stirred for a moment, then quiet ensued as all eyes turned with interest toward Pa.

"You all know how long we've been praying and searching for a preacher. It seemed like God raised one up right in our midst when Reverend Greene came back to Harper."

Tarah's gaze darted to Anthony. His face glowed red, and a look of dread covered his features.

"Now the reverend's the first to admit things started off a mite rough, but I think we all agree God has made quite a turnaround in our church in the past few weeks."

Heads nodded in approval. Mr. Tucker slapped Anthony on the back. "Doin' a fine job, Preacher."

Tarah's heart soared as she realized her pa was about to confirm Anthony's position as pastor. She glanced at Louisa, whose gaze was fixed on her new beau, her face glowing with the joy of newfound love.

Tarah bristled. Anthony should be sharing this moment with the person he loved. Instead he was about to be given the boot right out of Louisa's life. *Lord, it just isn't right. I know Anthony doesn't love me, but please don't let him be too hurt over Louisa.*

Without thought, she nudged Louisa. "Can't you wait until tomorrow, at least? Give Anthony this night to enjoy getting the permanent position."

"Too late," Louisa replied without averting her gaze from Tom Kirkpatrick. "I told Anthony during our last dance together."

Pa again lifted his arms to quiet the commotion brought on by his last statement. "I guess you've pretty much figured out what I'm going to say next. Come on up here, Reverend Greene, and let everyone have a good look at Harper's new pastor."

A wide grin split Anthony's achingly handsome face as he strode forward and stood before his friends, family, and congregation. Pa shook his hand vigorously. "Congratulations, Reverend. I pray you'll shepherd this flock with the compassion of David, the wisdom of Solomon, and the love and sacrifice of the Great Shepherd, Jesus Christ."

Tears sprang to Tarah's eyes even as Anthony smiled, his own eyes glistening in the lamplit room. "I thank you all for the trust you've placed in me. I ask that you pray for me as often as you will."

Pa stepped forward again and clapped Anthony on the shoulder. "I have one more announcement to make, then the band will play the last waltz of the night." He grinned at Anthony. "God has blessed our town with new folks moving in all the time, and we don't want it said we don't take good care of our preacher. So the town council has approved the building of a new church. And not a sod building, either."

A cheer rose up from the crowd. Pa waited for quiet to resume before continuing. "Mr. Thomas, our distinguished banker, has approved a loan and donated the first fifty dollars for shipping in enough wood for the church and a small parsonage."

Anthony's mouth dropped at the news, and everyone turned to the banker in a mix of disbelief and astonishment. Mrs. Thomas stood beside her husband, her chin lifted with pride, shoulders straight with the dignity this effort afforded them.

"You see what a generous man my father is?" Louisa asked smugly. "Now maybe the town will vote him onto the council."

"I hope so, Louisa." And Tarah was surprised to discover that she really did. Mr. Thomas was in a position to help the townsfolk, and a little mutual respect might be called for now that Harper was becoming a real town.

Anthony cleared his throat and inclined his head. "Again, I thank you folks and you, Mr. Thomas, for your generosity. I will try to earn your faith in me." With that, he shook Pa's hand again and stepped off the little platform as the band began to play a reel to start off the last waltz of the night.

Tarah found her gaze fixed on Anthony, her heart beating time to the reel. Unable to look away, she watched as he stopped to speak to well-wishers. Then in an instant, he found her. Tarah's breath caught in her throat at the intensity of his gaze, and she couldn't have looked away if she had wanted to. He strode toward her and smiled. "Will you give me the honor of the last dance, Miss St. John?"

Heart pounding, Tarah nodded and placed her hand in his. He pulled her as close as propriety allowed, but Tarah was sure he could feel her heartbeat as he swept her around the dance floor.

"Congratulations, Anthony," she said when she found her voice. "I'm so happy for you."

He grinned. "I was a little worried when your pa started off talking about how rough the first few weeks were. You don't know how relieved I was when he went on."

Tarah let out a giggle. "You should have seen your face."

"You were watching me?" His gaze searched her face.

She tried to think of a flippant answer, but nothing came, so she simply nodded. He drew a quick breath, his eyes serious. "Tarah," he said hesitantly, "now that my future is secure in Harper and we're building a parsonage, I'll be in a position to marry and settle down."

Tarah's heart plummeted. Maybe he didn't understand Louisa's change in affections after all. "Oh, Anthony —"

"Now wait. Before you say anything, I know you're planning to go to Starling in another month or so, and I wouldn't try to stop you if that's really what you want to do."

A frown furrowed Tarah's brow as Louisa's words came back to taunt her. *I wouldn't be surprised if he turns to you before the evening is over.*

"Why are you looking at me like that?" Anthony asked. "All I'm asking for is a chance to court you like a gentleman." He sent her a heart-stopping grin, which only fueled Tarah's anger.

She stopped midstep, then winced as Anthony stumbled and ground his boot into her slipper-clad foot.

Suddenly the air in the room was stifling, and Tarah's chest heaved, her palms growing moist. Without a word, she glared at Anthony and stomped as best she could with a limp toward the door. She snatched her coat from a peg on the wall, and brushing past Pa and Cassidy, she hurried out the door, desperate for a private spot where she could spill the threatening tears.

"Tarah, wait." At Anthony's voice, she spun around to find not only Anthony staring at her, but Pa and Cassidy and Mrs. Greene.

"What happened, Tarah?" Cassidy asked. "Is something wrong with your foot?"

"What? Oh, Anthony stepped on it. But I'm fine."

"Then why are you so upset, honey?" Pa asked.

Heaving a frustrated sigh, Tarah glanced at Anthony to see if he would speak up and admit what he had done. The look of bewilderment on his face boiled her blood.

She knit her brows together and took a step closer to him. "Ask him!" she said, never taking her gaze from Anthony's face.

"Anthony, what have you done?" Mrs. Greene's voice trembled.

"Is there something we should discuss in

private, son?" Pa asked, a hard edge to his voice that Tarah had rarely heard.

"I — I'm not sure, sir. All I said was —"

Tarah had had all she could take. After months of dreaming about him, she'd had to watch Louisa hook him, then throw him back. After the heartbreak of releasing him to God, now he asked her for permission to come calling!

She took another step closer to Anthony until they were close enough to touch. "All he said was that he wanted to court me! Can you believe that, Ma? After all this time? Now he wants to court me!"

A look of faint amusement covered Cassidy's features. She opened her mouth, then closed it again and shook her head as Tarah continued to rant.

"After mooning over Louisa Thomas for as long as I've known him, he suddenly wants to court me. And do you know why, Mrs. Greene?"

"You're a very pretty girl, Tarah," she replied, the same look of amusement on her face. "Anthony has always thought very highly of you."

"Ha!" Tarah let out an unladylike snort and turned to Pa, knowing she could count on him to understand. "The reason he suddenly wants to court me is because Louisa threw him over for that university fellow tonight."

"That's not exactly —"

"Oh, Anthony," Tarah said, her energy suddenly drained, "you're not going to deny it?"

"Tarah, please." Louisa's voice broke through the silence that had suddenly permeated the tension-filled air. "Keep your voice down before the whole town hears you make fools of all of us."

Tarah spun around and glared at Louisa. "What are you doing out here?"

"Tom and I came out to get a breath of air."

"And you decided to eavesdrop?" Sarcasm dripped from Tarah's lips.

Louisa scowled. "It isn't as though I had to struggle to hear you hollering at poor Anthony."

"Poor Anthony? As if you care about his feelings," Tarah snapped, her gaze darting to the young man holding protectively to Louisa's elbow.

"Dell, perhaps we should leave these young people to work all this out between them," Cassidy suggested quietly.

"No!" Tarah said, keeping her gaze fixed on Louisa. "I want you to stay."

Louisa glanced nervously about the little

gathering. "I'm afraid this misunderstanding is all my fault."

Tarah's mouth dropped open as she stared at the contrite face that only a moment before she would have loved to slap. Louisa gave a resigned sigh and continued. "It's true I cared for Anthony a great deal — or thought I did," she added, smiling at Tom. "But as kind as he has always been, he never felt the same way about me."

"But I thought —"

"You thought what I led you to believe," Louisa said, a wry grin twisting her lips. "But Anthony had nothing to do with it. I'm sure you remember the night we both had dinner at the Greenes'?"

Tarah nodded, reliving the humiliation.

"Anthony told me that night that he is not in love with me and never could be because he's in love with someone else — you. He only brought me to the dance instead of you because I begged him not to humiliate me in front of the whole town."

Eyes widening, Tarah's gaze darted to Anthony, who stared at Louisa in astonishment.

"And, Anthony," Louisa said, "I think you'll find the feeling is returned."

Pa snickered behind them, adding to Tarah's humiliation. So much for understanding.

"Dell," Cassidy admonished.

Tarah planted her hands on her hips and struggled to maintain her composure. "Now hold on, Louisa Thomas. Who do you think you are to speak for me?"

Completely unintimidated, Louisa lifted a brow and smirked. "Come now, Tarah. We're all being honest here. If I can humiliate myself with the truth, why can't you? And if the truth be told, all this is your fault to begin with."

Tarah gasped. "Mine? You just admitted it was yours."

Her slim shoulders lifted. "I've changed my mind. If you had let Anthony know how you feel about him in the first place, you would have been the one to go with him on all the picnics and horseback rides. And you would have come with him to the dance instead of me. Then all of this could have been avoided. But you have your pride, don't you?" She smiled up at her escort. "Shall we go, Tom? I think I've done all I can do here."

Tarah watched them leave arm in arm. Her mind whirled, trying to absorb the shocking revelations of the past few minutes. Anthony loved her? But what about the lessons she had learned about letting God direct her life? Was it even possible that Anthony was hers all along? Then it struck her. She had let him go, and God had given him back. It had been a hard lesson to learn, but she knew she was stronger spiritually as a result than she ever could have been without learning to surrender her will to God's.

Her anger drained away as she turned slowly and caught her breath at the intensity of Anthony's gaze. He stepped forward and took her hands, and everything and everyone present faded away.

Pa cleared his throat, making them both jump. "I still expect you to court my daughter properly, young man."

"Yes, sir," Anthony said without removing his gaze from Tarah's.

"Then I suppose we can go now. Unless you want us to stay, Tarah?"

"No, Pa. You can go."

"Ladies?" he said, turning to Cassidy and Mrs. Greene. "Shall we return to the dance?"

Tarah could hear them laughing as they strolled away, but she didn't care. All that mattered was knowing Anthony shared her feelings and that her love for him was part of God's plan all along.

She stared at him, not daring to speak for

fear it had all been a dream that would float away if she broke the silence.

Anthony searched her face, his warm hands still enclosing hers. He drew a ragged breath and tightened his grip. "Do you love me?"

"Do *you* love me?" Tarah whispered.

Anthony's lips curved into a wry grin. "I've been trying to tell you for weeks how much I care about you."

"You have?"

He nodded. "Remember me telling you I'd do anything for you? I even offered to marry you, but you didn't think I was serious. I love you." He paused. "Now you. Was Louisa speaking the truth?"

Heat rushed to Tarah's cheeks. She dropped her chin and nodded. "Yes, it's true."

Releasing a sigh, Anthony pulled her closer.

Tarah met his gaze head-on and held her breath.

"I want to ask you to marry me. Do you think your pa would give his blessing without a courtship? Because I'm willing to wait however long it takes, but I'd prefer to be married as soon as the parsonage is built."

Amusement washed over Tarah, and she tilted her head to one side, a grin tugging at the corners of her lips. "Have I ever told you how Pa and Cassidy met?"

A frown furrowed Anthony's brow. "No. Do you want to tell me right now?"

Tarah giggled and nodded. "My pa placed an advertisement for a wife. Cassidy answered, and they married less than three weeks later with no courting whatsoever. And I've never seen two people more in love. Have you?"

His lips twitched. "Now that you mention it, I haven't."

"So you see, I don't think my pa or Cassidy will raise any objections to our marriage."

"Are you saying yes?"

"Yes, Anthony." Tarah closed her eyes as his head descended, and she knew this time she was going to be kissed. At the first touch of his lips on hers, Tarah wrapped her arms about his neck. The gentle caress sent shivers down her spine as she gave herself over to the heady sensations filling her for the first time.

Just as Anthony drew her closer and deepened the kiss, a sudden thought popped into her mind. She gasped, tearing her mouth away. He drew back immediately as her eyes flew open.

"What is it?" He shook his head. "I'm

sorry. I should never have been so forward."

"No, Anthony. Of course I welcomed your kiss. It isn't that."

"Then what is it, sweetheart?"

Tarah drew a steadying breath and regarded him frankly, feeling her heart racing within her chest. "When I marry, Laney and Ben come with me. And I don't want a man who puts up with them but secretly resents them. They need a good man in their life — someone who will love them. Otherwise, they'd be better off with no man at all."

Relief washed over Anthony's face, and he smiled, pulling her close once again. "I know those children are part of the deal. And I wouldn't have it any other way. But do you think they'll want me in their lives?"

"I think so. Ben idolizes you already, and Laney's coming around."

"That's a good thing," Anthony said with a teasing smile. " 'Cause I don't stay where I ain't wanted."

Anthony's head descended once again, and his lips captured Tarah's, muffling the sound of their laughter.

ABOUT THE AUTHOR

Tracey V. Bateman lives in Missouri with her husband and their four children. She counts on her relationship with God to bring balance to her busy life. Grateful for God's many blessings, Tracey believes she is living proof that "all things are possible to them that believe," and she happily encourages anyone who will listen to dream big and see where God will take them.